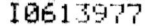
Crabapple Court

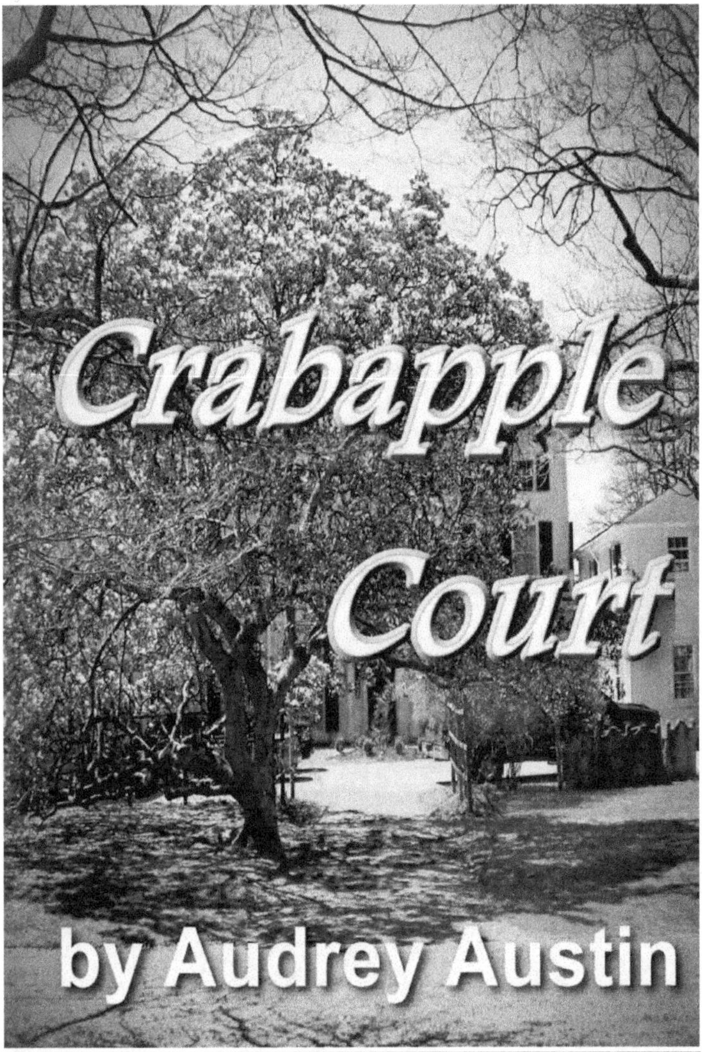

by Audrey Austin

CRABAPPLE COURT

A novella

by

Audrey Austin

CRABAPPLE COURT

audrey@persona.ca

http://www.amazon.com/author/audreyaustin

http://www.facebook.com/audreyaustinca

http://yuneekpix.com

Cover Design by Susan Ruby K.

CRABAPPLE COURT

Crabapple Court – a novella

is dedicated with love to

my brother, Kenneth Lester Austin

who at an early age

set the bar high for the rest of us

by his fine example

of strength and leadership.

OTHER BOOKS
BY AUDREY AUSTIN

Sara. a Canadian Saga

Reawakening

The Silent Star plus a Dozen

Keeping It Simple

Ellen and The Hummingtree

Moose Road – a Canadian Tragedy

Beyond The Blue

Recompense

When God Gives Us Spring

Social Studies – Book One

Social Studies – Book Two

Social Studies – Book Three

Stories for Children: The Last Drop &

At The Edge of His World

Short Stories – too numerous to list

http://www.amazon.com/author/audreyaustin

TABLE OF CONTENTS

TABLE OF CONTENTS (cont.)

ONE

CRABAPPLE COURT

ONE:

Police Chief Madison Morris

This case beats all! Yes, sir! This case sure does beat all!

My name is Madison Morris and I have been Chief of Police in our little Town of Fairmont for nearly twenty years. Some would say that is probably way too many. I have my days, especially recently, when I'm inclined to agree with them. As you might imagine being a cop in a small town means that I have lots of stories to tell; that is if I had a mind to tell them. But most of them wouldn't be of much interest and they sure would not hold too much of anyone's attention.

It's true that even peaceful Fairmont has its share of petty crime. People running stop signs and neighbours fighting over fence lines wastes a lot of my time. It's no fun but I'm sorry to say that even in what appears to be a peaceful corner of God's good earth I've had to deal with too many cases of domestic abuse. Our pretty little oasis has even been known to have some break and enters. But, truth be told, most of my time is spent ticketing speeders and characters who think they know how to park a car.

But that was then. This is now.

The whole world is bending an ear to hear about this one. Yes, sir, this case beats all. Yes, this one sure beats all.

Like I said my name is Madison Morris but most of my friends just call me Maddy. At one time when I was younger, just after doing a stint in the Canadian Forces, I was hired and kept busy working as a Police Constable in the City of Toronto. There is big time crime in the city: murder, robbery, drug trafficking just to mention a few. I found the work stressful after a few years. I couldn't seem to turn it off and I was bringing my work home with me. This was bad enough but worse than that my wife started finding it stressful having to put up with me and all my worrying and grumbling.

So I applied for a posting and I confess I was relieved to be hired as a Constable by the Town of Fairmont. I worked hard, kept my nose clean and it did not take me long to climb the short ladder of small town success. It was a welcome change in my lifestyle when I was promoted and made the transition to Chief of Police. That was more than fifteen years ago. My life is much calmer now and my wife is much happier.

We bought a little bungalow on a quiet side street in town and in no time at all my wife became involved in community affairs. She joined a book club, a little amateur theatre group and the local Methodist Church. She sings alto in the choir and she goes to some women's group that meets once a month to talk about how they can raise money for new pots and pans or new curtains for the church basement hall. Usually it's a soup luncheon and it's not that I mind eating soup but after a couple of years I began to think that the women's group could use some new members with a little more imagination.

Anyway all these activities keep my wife, Evelyn, happy. More importantly they keep her off my back. This suits me just fine. I have no interest in church myself but she drags me along every Sunday morning. I'd rather stay home to sleep in but to keep peace in the family I allow myself to be dragged.

When I'm not working I like to watch the football on TV or the hockey or whatever sport is in season. I also like to read stories; mystery stories mostly. Those murder mystery stories bring some excitement into my often boring life.

There's not a lot of excitement in my job. I spend most of my time either sitting behind my desk at the police station at the far end of Fairmont's Main Street or behind the wheel of the black Chevy Impala with its impressive lettering on its front doors. Sometimes I sit there for hours looking for speeders and parking violators.

I'm not the only paid police officer in Fairmont. I work with Constable Nick Taylor. He's been on the Fairmont force for more than five years now. We work well together. Maybe once a month we spend a bit of time together over a beer in Alice's Café on Main Street. We don't socialize together much though because I've got a good twenty years on him. Apart from work we don't have a heck of a lot in common. But he's a good man; smart and reliable.

Our working world turned upside down two days ago. It started with a phone call from a fellow who said his name is Gerald Gagnon. Sounding cool as a cucumber he says, "My grandchild is missing."

That telephone call was the beginning. Now the quiet, peaceful Town of Fairmont has turned into a ten ring circus. Our usually ignored local newspaper is making a roaring trade. The story has even been picked up by the big newspaper fellows in Toronto. These days I can't get a seat in Alice's café. The place is filled with newspaper reporters. Kind of a double-edged sword! Tragic circumstances for one grieving family sure are good for business!

I'm going to tell this story in the best way I know how but there was a lot going on inside those big houses on Crabapple Court that I didn't know about.   I didn't hesitate to put in a call for help when the situation started getting out of hand. The OPP were there for me and it wasn't long before the RCMP had a hand out demanding a piece of the pie.

TWO

TWO:

Where is Susie Donnelly?

Word started to get around once the headline of the little known but soon to be world-renowned Fairmont Times simply whispered the question, *Where is Susan Donnelly?* Before long this matter of concern was hanging off the tongue of every student, working man and coffee klatching housewife in Fairmont.

In all my years as Chief of Police in Fairmont this was the first time a local crime got attention and hit the headlines of the big Toronto newspapers. "FEAR IN FAIRMONT!" the Toronto Star screamed while the Globe and Mail's more sedate headline declared *CRIME IN CRABAPPLE COURT.* Our local paper simply persisted in asking the question, "*Where is Susan Donnelly?*"

It is now a question lurking in the minds of everyone. Just like I've told you, Fairmont is a quiet little town. Sure, it has its fair share of vandals and, sure, we never grow tired of handing out as many speeding tickets as possible but before now crime has never expanded outside or beyond the petty category. Children play happily, freely and safely in the backyards, parks and playgrounds of Fairmont. Of course it is safe. Fairmont has always been a safe place. Who could ever imagine a child's disappearance? It's unthinkable! Who knew such a tragedy could occur? Indeed, who knew? I listen to all the prattle of the townsfolk.

"Never would have guessed," says one.

"Not in a million years," says another.

The residents of Fairmont are simply surprised and shocked.

"Surely not in Fairmont! This is the kind of thing that goes on in Toronto or Montreal!"

"Yes, and even worse in Detroit or New York City!"

"Can't believe something like this happened in Fairmont. Especially on Crabapple Court!"

"Yes, especially on Crabapple Court! Never would have guessed."

Everybody knows that Crabapple Court is one of the finest streets in the small Ontario town of Fairmont. It is a street lined with beautiful executive homes and its prime location close to all the amenities Fairmont has to offer could not be more convenient for the families resident on this prestigious street.

With its mature Crabapple trees lining the boulevard; its wide, red, interlock brick sidewalks; its closeness to good public school, and library; not to mention the Fairmont Methodist Church right on its corner, Crabapple Court is in a most convenient location. It is in close proximity and within walking distance to Main Street shopping.

If you were to turn right at the church and walk along the sidewalk on one side of Main Street you would pass Denny's Delicatessen; the dress shop run by Doris Shannon and her sister Irene; the Buck or Two Store; Arnone's Fruit and Vegetable market and Bob's Bakery where residents buy their fresh bread each day and the fancy decorated cakes for special occasions.

Crossing the street to the other side at the town's only traffic light you would travel past the No Frills Supermarket; Best Bob Beauty Salon; Victor's Barber Shop and the Shoppers' Drugmart; not to mention Alice's Café where the young housewives love to meet for coffee and gossip while their children attend the Fairmont Elementary School.

No one questions the fact that Crabapple Court is considered the most desirable street in town. Everybody wants to live there but everyone knows that in order to do so one would need to be either very affluent or possess a willingness to be up to the eyeballs in debt. Most Fairmont residents are not so willing. And it is a fact that most residents would not even qualify for such a monstrous mortgage. Fairmont residents in general are far from affluent. Simple hardworking people, most feel content and happy as they live a quiet family life within the comfort of their modest bungalows or apartments.

The owners of the luxury homes on Crabapple Court are a tiny minority in Fairmont's population. If not wealthy they are, without exception, financially comfortable individuals: yuppies for the most part.

There are only five houses situated on Crabapple Court. These five houses, numbered three, five, seven, nine and eleven, line only one side of the wide street while on the other side is the wooden boardwalk that snakes its way from one end of the pretty, public, soft sand beach to the other. At the road's edge and in front of the boardwalk are several parking spots for Fairmont residents who come to Crabapple Court throughout the summer to enjoy the beach and the fine, pristine lake swimming.

On Crabapple Court the five executive homes occupy as much land space as is easily filled in other areas of the little town by at least ten dwellings much more modest in size and design. Each two acre lot has a professionally landscaped front yard with flower-lined pathway and neatly trimmed bushes and hedges. The manicured front lawns seem to stretch for miles before passing the Crabapple trees and reaching the brightly painted front doors of the huge, custom built, luxury homes.

Each house boasts an even greater backyard, each with swimming pool of course, and there are a couple of yards which also contain a private tennis court.

At the foot of each front yard is the town's interlocking red brick sidewalk and on the other side of the sidewalk is the wide boulevard. Several of the homes have large Crabapple trees on the front lawns and the Town of Fairmont, in its wisdom, planted more Crabapple trees on the boulevard. It was for this reason inevitable that the small street would be aptly named Crabapple Court.

There are few plants that create greater visual impact during Ontario's all four seasons than the flowering Crabapple which is often called the *Jewel of the Landscape.* In the harshness of a cold Canadian winter the soft snow accents the bare branches and the tree's satisfying shape. In autumn the Crabapple foliage and fruit are vibrant. The falling leaves reveal the glorious colour of the fruit which is borne in the summer and in the fall.

It is during the spring of the year that the Crabapple begins to flower. The delicate colours offered by emerging leaves and buds entice the eye of the tourist's camera. While unopened flower buds hint of one colour, other hues are revealed in a spectacular floral display. Once the flowers are open they are, like the residents of Crabapple Court, vulnerable to the elements and hopeful of a long and pleasing life.

In this fashion Crabapple Court is the only street in Fairmont that is lined with these *jewels*. The boulevards of the five houses are deep and very long. Each boulevard boasts several Crabapple trees and they provide an attractive and an ongoing all-season draw for camera-carrying tourists. Most often these visitors are spotted by the locals in the spring and early summer of each year when the pearly white to delicate pink to deep red blossoms have almost completed their journey toward full bloom.

These beautiful eye-catching trees do their best to hide the five houses from the curious eyes of the Fairmont residents as well as from those of the tourists who walk their dogs, their children; not to mention their jealousies, along the boardwalk on the fair weather days.

If one were to view only these five homes he might imagine he was looking at the homes of movie stars in California. Indeed, by viewing only these houses, it becomes difficult to imagine that Fairmont is a small, struggling mill town but that is exactly what it is.

However even a town such as this requires professional people to serve the community. Every town needs a doctor, a veterinarian, a lawyer, an investment banker, and a dentist. Fairmont is no exception and in addition to these professionals Fairmont, being a one-industry town, is home to the mill's owner who just happens to own the only hotel and most of the small business establishments that hug the sidewalks along Main Street. It is not surprising and in fact it is expected that, indeed, there will be some, if not many, upper scale homes found in a lunch-bucket town which will suit the needs of these upwardly mobile professionals.

Without exception the residents of Crabapple Court do not like to draw attention to themselves or to their homes. I know for a fact that they do not like publicity. No, sir, they do not appreciate media attention but this day, whether they like it or not, the Fairmont residents are keeping them under strict scrutiny. Indeed the eyes of the entire country are fixed upon them.

Just as the branches of the flowering Crabapple trees reach for the freedom of their future the townsfolk imagine that the little girl's arms are doing likewise. Who can bear to imagine that the child may be dead? It is hoped that the missing child is somewhere in captivity; that a ransom will be sought; that the little girl will remain unharmed. But young mothers in town cannot rid their minds of the disturbing picture of a missing child who may be crying out in the darkness for her rescue, for her safety, for her mother.

The child, it is reported, is barely four feet tall while the Crabapple trees achieve a height of nearly twenty-five feet. If one were to stand in the centre of this street called Crabapple Court the eye would be excited to capture the beauty of the bountiful benefactors.

To see beyond the trees, well, there lies the dichotomy, the contrast, the difficulty and the puzzle to be solved. Those who tread the boardwalk strain their eyes but to no avail. They cannot see the five houses with any clarity. They can only imagine what goes on behind those very attractive closed doors and imagine they do. Fairmont residents are dazed. Mothers hold their children close while fathers give them stern warnings not to roam from what had always been considered the safety of their backyard.

Yes, I hear them.

"Don't let go of my hand," a parent warns.

"No, you can't go to the movies. I've told you that you are to stay in the backyard!" another orders.

The children of Fairmont sense the panic of their parents and they become fearful. "What happened?" They want to know.

Parents hesitate to answer. They wonder how they can keep the children safe without instilling fear in their hearts. How can they offer a reassuring answer to the children when in their own worried minds they have only unanswered questions?

And I listen to the children. I hear them talk amongst themselves.

"Susie is missing," says one.

"She ran away," says another.

"Is she dead?" one asks.

"Shhh," the parents caution. "Come inside now children. This is not a good day to be outside playing."

"Why do we have to come in?"

"It's not raining," another child cries.

And the mother raises her eyes as with unaccustomed caution she looks up and down the street on which she lives before she says "Hush now, come in child. Don't ask so many questions. Come into the house now"

"But Mom."

"No buts about it! Just do as you're told!"

It is not only the children of Fairmont asking the questions. No, indeed. Questions bounce around town. Is it a kidnap? Is it murder?

The little Town of Fairmont is bursting at the seams with intruders; some welcome and some not so welcome. It is unheard of but true that the town's only hotel has no vacancy. Alice's café business has never been this busy. Ka-ching! Ka-ching! Small business owners experiencing a big leap in sales try not to reveal their secret pleasure at this money-making dilemma.

Out-of-town big city reporters have arrived and they ask the questions. Me and my partner, we ask the questions. Soon the RCMP fellows are asking the questions. School teachers ask the questions. I know that they feel grateful that school is out for the summer. I heard one teacher say to another that he wonders how he will answer the questions of his fearful students once the school bell rings to start another academic year in September.

Everyone has a question. Most are convinced the ugly answer is deeply hidden somewhere behind the concealing beauty of the Crabapple trees.

Who knew that such evil doings could hide behind such an attractive, extravagant façade? Newspapers are read. Everyone knows there had been no sign of a break-in. No alarms were sounded. There was no child's cry in the night. This could not be the work of an outsider. No, indeed, the public insists, "The culprit lives in one of those houses!"

"But which house?"

"Well, there's only five. It shouldn't take the cops long to figure it out. There's not a single doubt the evil-doer lurks within one of these five homes."

"Then why haven't they arrested someone?"

"They will. Give it time. Rest assured they will."

"But the child … "

"Yes, poor child."

"Innocent lamb."

"If only I could get my hands on the monster that did this thing!"

In this way the fears, the questions and the threats shared among the shocked residents of Fairmont abound throughout these summer days stealing the reckless fun and freedom of the children who want to play from sunrise to sundown as children have always done since time immemorial during school's summer vacation.

"It shouldn't take them long to figure it out. Only five houses."

Yes, but which house indeed. We sure do have our work cut out for us and I've done enough talking. It's time for me to get to work. I will let this story tell itself.

THREE

THREE:

The Homes on Crabapple Court

The Fairmont Methodist Church with its imposing tall steeple reaching for the heavens takes up the entirety of the very large city property situate at the corner of Main Street and Crabapple Court. On Sunday mornings it is the custom of the parishioners to park their vehicles in the paved parking lot provided for their use behind the church. This lot neighbours the high, well-fenced side of the first house that faces with pride the lakeside boardwalk.

In spite of this security fence it would not be impossible for one so inclined to climb over and make his way through the backyards of the Crabapple Court homes.

"Did he get in the back way?" one asks.

"No, no! The culprit lives in one of those houses!"

"What makes you so sure of that?"

"Mark my words! It's one of those rich perverts!"

"Pervert? The child is kidnapped by a pervert?"

"I'd bet my bottom dollar on it!"

"But the guy could have gone in the back way."

"He lives in one of those houses I'm telling you!"

"But which house?"

"The cops will figure it out! Could be any one of them!"

The front of this massive first house has very large, arched Palladian windows on both the first and second storeys allowing the occupant an outstanding view of the Crabapple blossoms and the lake beyond. There are large windows on the rear of this house as well but it is a fact that no report of a prowler has been made.

On Crabapple Court there is no house numbered One. Townsfolk say this is because not one person is willing to allow his neighbour to be number one.

"So into themselves," says one.

"They all want to be number one," says another.

Ego rules and for this reason the Town assigned the number to no one.

Consequently the first house on Crabapple Court is numbered three. This home is the prized possession of Ernie and his wife, Doctor Heather

Martin. Ernie Martin is a lawyer whose law office, aptly named Martin Law Firm even though he is the only member of the company, is situated upstairs on the second floor above Arnone's Fruit and Vegetable Market on Fairmont's Main Street.

Ernie and Heather met many years ago at the University of Toronto. She was in her first year of medical school when she met her husband who was two years her senior. He was also two years ahead of her in school and already comfortably established in his law office at the time of her graduation from medical school. Heather and Ernie dated for a few years. She made the move from Toronto to Fairmont to be close to him. She was welcomed by the townspeople who are always in need of another physician. Heather practiced medicine in the small Fairmont Hospital.

Ernie and Heather married. Years pass and now they live together in their house with their three teenaged sons. Their first born is William who is seventeen. Next in line is Harold who is fifteen. Then there is Gordon, the thirteen year old baby who is ready to start his first year of high school once July says hello to September.

Ernie and Heather are people who like to do all things in a sensible, logical and predictable order or so it seems on the surface.

**

Living next door to the Martins at Number Five Crabapple Court is Patricia Donnelly. Like her neighbour Heather, Patricia is also a medical doctor. Unlike her neighbour who lives happily with her husband, Patricia is a widow. Her husband died two years prior from lung cancer. Especially because she is a physician it broke her heart that she was unable to find a way to save him from the cruel, fatal disease. He was a young man; only thirty-seven years old at the time of his death. He was well-known as a successful architect who designed their Queen Anne Style home with its many gables and large wrap-around verandah.

The widowed Patricia is a doctor, a healer, but often in her loneliness she will whisper, *"Physician, heal thyself."* In spite of her thriving, busy medical private practice she is often lonesome and bereft. She misses her husband and grieves for his loss. She holds her only child, seven-year-old Susan, close to her heart but, as of that dreadful, hot summer day, no longer physically close.

"Oh, my God! Susan, where are you?"

She awakens that miserable morning to discover that her little girl's bed is empty. Yes, the sheets are rumpled and the bed has been obviously slept in but Susie is nowhere to be found in or about the large house. Not knowing where to turn Patricia tries to phone her father, Gerald. His phone rings several times at his Elliot Lake home with no answer. Frantic, she dials again but with no success.

Then she thinks of his cabin by the lake and that is where she finds him. She reaches him on his cell phone.

It is still early in the morning when Gerald answers the phone. "Slow down, Patricia! I can barely understand what you are saying."

"I can't find Susie! Dad, you have to come!"

"I'm on my way," he promises.

Gerald Gagnon makes one quick phone call to his neighbour and is assured that she will keep an eye on his house while he's away. She asks a favour; one to which he does not hesitate to agree. After scribbling down an address he ends the phone conversation.

It will be a long drive but he gets into his black Jeep Grand Cherokee and begins his journey to Crabapple Court. He leaves directly from his hunting cabin on the lakeside property. Although he is not far from his house in The City of Elliot Lake he doesn't take the time to go there in order to pack some clothing. He doesn't want to waste any more precious time and besides he hopes there will be no need for him to stay in Fairmont for more than a day or so. He is on the road, his only desire to be with his daughter.

Gerald Gagnon is the only family Patricia has left. Being an only child she misses her mother who suffered a major heart attack and died when

Patricia was just a child. Losing her mother at such an early age and losing her husband too quickly has taught Patricia to keep her suffering silent and deep within.

Heart pounding, she scours the house. She has already experienced too much loss! She cannot bear another.

"Susan, stop hiding! It's not funny! Susan, where are you?" she cries as she wanders from one room to another searching throughout the entire big house.

When he arrives at her home Gerald finds his daughter in a babbling state of hysteria as she sits curled into herself upon the living-room chesterfield. Not knowing what else to do he calls the Fairmont Hospital and talks to Doctor Heather Martin, his daughter's next door neighbour. Heather wastes no time in giving the injection which promptly puts Patricia to sleep. At Heather's urging, Gerald then calls the local police.

***

Number Seven Crabapple Court is the home of Marsha and Daniel Kovacs. Their house is a stately white Georgian home designed with a centre hall plan. Its big front door looks splendid in the centre of the house and it is elegantly adorned with black shuttered windows on either side. More shuttered windows line up like soldiers in a neat row across the front of the dwelling's second storey.

Daniel is a dentist with his dental office on Main Street. His wife, Marsha Kovacs, is a psychospiritual practitioner who carries on a successful private therapy practice in her home's basement office. Daniel and Marsha have no children. They live a quiet, respectable life, or so it seems to a casual observer. Together they attend the Methodist Church each Sunday morning. Marsha attends choir practice every Thursday evening and she sings a lovely soprano in the church choir during Sunday morning worship services.

She has always wanted a child but now at the age of forty-two she struggles to accept the fact that it is never going to happen. The reality of the situation is that she is never going to give birth; never going to have a child of her own. In years past she had been open to adopting a child but her husband, Daniel, was adamant in his refusal to consider the option.

"You are all I need," he assures his wife.

But Marsha needs more. Some say this is why she returns to college later in life while in her thirties in order to become a psychotherapist. She could mother her clients if she so chose. "But," others ask after the child's disappearance, "what kind of crazy people has she been bringing into the neighbourhood? Who are these looney tunes that are coming to her home office for counseling; for psychotherapy?"

"Who knows who these people are and why they need help?"

"How do we know Marsha didn't steal the child? It's common knowledge she wants a child. Everyone knows how desperately she has always wanted a child of her own."

"No, not Marsha! Bet it is one of the nuts that come to her for counseling."

"Well, maybe it could be her but I doubt it."

"Me too! I'll put my money on one of those crazies. Who wants to make a bet?"

And so the townspeople talk.

***

Number Nine Crabapple Court is the home of George Cavendish and his wife, Marian. The people say George owns Fairmont.

"There's not a pie he hasn't got his finger in," one says.

"Tightwad," another exclaims.

"Yeah, but his wife is nice," is often repeated.

George owns the Cavendish Paper Mill which is the only industry in town. George, a smart fellow who hates to part with money, makes sure he spends it wisely. He bought many residential properties that he keeps tenanted and he owns more than half the commercial buildings that line Main Street, not to mention the two big apartment buildings and the only movie theatre in Fairmont.

His wife, Marian, is a stay-at-home mother of three children who are now all old enough to be attending school. The youngest is eight year old Robert and he misses his playmate, Susie. "Did she run away, Mom?" he asks his mother.

"Why such a question, Robert?" Marian replies. "Why on earth would a little girl run away from such a lovely family?"

"She didn't have no family. All she had is a mother," Robert answers.

"She has a grandfather who visits."

"Yeah, but Susie told me she doesn't like her grandfather. She said he is kind of weird."

Next in line in the Cavendish family is Dolores who at sixteen will be going into grade eleven. Robert and Dolores are popular yet well-behaved children who enjoy their friendships and their family life in Fairmont.

The same cannot be said for the oldest Cavendish child. Thomas, at nineteen, is well-known to the local police. He has committed no serious crimes to anyone's knowledge but he spends too much time in the local pool hall, drinking too much beer and smoking too much of something illegal. More recently he has taken to hanging around the elementary school playground. Why is he doing this? No one knows for sure. Unlike his parents, Tom is reckless, irresponsible and a great worry to his mother who prays for his redemption every Sunday morning in the Methodist Church on the corner.

Like its neighbours the Cavendish house sits on a large property. Originally it is a modern ranch style bungalow but as the children keep arriving additions are built. The first addition transforms the bungalow to a two storey house. The second is an addition to the side of the house bringing their home closer to the property line they share with their neighbours, the Kovacs.

The third addition is a large verandah that circles the entire house and this is where much of the family's outdoor living takes place. There is a garden swing on the verandah and there are many garden chairs distributed here and there on the verandah. There is a card table set up with four metal folding chairs gathered around it; a great place for the family to get together to play their board games.

"Best money I ever spent!" George Cavendish is often heard to exclaim. Yes, this third addition is one that is well utilized by all members of the Cavendish family.

The construction of the three additions takes place over a number of years and leaves the home with no particular style that one could put a finger on. "Kind of an odd looking place," some have been known to say.

***

The last house on Crabapple Court is Number Eleven, the home of wealthy investment banker, Mario Colletti. With its large white pillars over the massive front entrance and its multi-paned windows it is in the style characteristic of a Colonial Revival home.

Unlike her husband, Mario's wife, Annette, comes from humble beginnings. Before their marriage she was steadily employed as a sales clerk in the Town of Fairmont's only small department store. This is the store where Mario likes to buy his clothes because they are inexpensive. Mario has lots of money but the truth of the matter is that he does not like to part with it. *Cheapskate* is a word that well-describes his spending habits.

Some say he chose Annette to be his bride because she comes from a working class background. Foolish man! He thinks her upbringing combined with her low income is a guarantee that after marriage she will continue to be low maintenance. He thinks she will share his miserly lifestyle and have no interest in his money. This does not turn out to be the case.

Mario and Annette have two children, both girls, who by now have married and moved away from Fairmont. Mario likes to brag about his family's success. That is how it has become common knowledge that they both live in fine homes in Mississauga which is part of the Greater Toronto Area better known as the GTA.

Both daughters have been blessed with children. Mario and Annette have five grandchildren and, much to Mario's chagrin, Annette has a passion for shopping and buying gifts for these grandchildren.

Now that they are empty-nesters the house is far too big for just the two of them. Annette has been known to tell friends that the rooms have become hollow. And now that she and her husband are growing older it is difficult for Annette to take care of the upkeep on such a large house on her own without help as she had been most capable to do during the earlier years of her marriage when her two children were growing up.

To make life easier for Annette, they hire a housekeeper with the name of Annie Benjamin. Annie is a young, pretty black woman who works hard and keeps the house in an immaculate condition. Annette soon learns that Annie's boyfriend does not always appreciate her the way any woman deserves to be appreciated. This lack of appreciation is sometimes made evident by a bruise on the arm or a scratch on the face.

And now you know that in this way the five houses on Crabapple Court are occupied. Fairmont residents are certain the kidnapper, or please God not the killer, lives in or is in some way connected to one of these houses.

"The cops have their job cut out for them," one resident says.

"How tough can it be?" another asks. "They just need to find a motive."

"Yes, sir, once they find a motive they will have their man!"

"What makes you so sure the kidnapper isn't a woman?"

"Oh, never thought of that."

And in this way the residents talk over the back fences throughout the town. "Yes, he's definitely in one of those houses." They all agree.

"But which house?"

"Yes, that remains the question."

FOUR

FOUR:

#3 – The Martin family

Heather Martin is busy working. She is shuffling papers on the desk in her office at the hospital when the phone rings. It is nearly two p.m. in the afternoon when she receives the surprising call from Gerald Gagnon. "Heather, I need your help. You must come quickly," he orders. "Patricia is hysterical and I've tried but I cannot calm her down."

"Hysterical? What's happened, Gerald? Why is she so upset?"

"Please, Heather. I have no time to answer your questions now. Please come right away. I am begging you."

After speaking with Gerald, Heather hangs up the phone with a sigh. She knows what she has to do. She looks with chagrin at the files on her desk. So many patients have afternoon appointments to see her but, though feeling slightly annoyed by the unwelcome interruption, she knows that she cannot disappoint Gerald. She cannot ignore her friend, Patricia, who, according to Gerald, is obviously experiencing some sort of trauma.

Patricia is not just one of Heather's co-workers at the hospital. She is also her next door neighbour and she counts herself as a friend.

"Cancel the rest of today's appointments, Roberta," she throws over her shoulder to the receptionist as she proceeds past her desk on her way out of the office and out of the hospital. In the parking lot she quickly walks to her car.

It is a short drive from the hospital to Crabapple Court. Heather parks her car in her own driveway before walking across the Donnelly's front lawn to Patricia's front door. She reaches out to ring the doorbell and within seconds Gerald is there urging her to hurry.

"Come in, Heather. I've tried but it's impossible to calm her down."

Heather finds Patricia in the living-room. She is huddled in a corner of the sofa. Her mournful cries are endless. "*My baby, I want my baby*," she keeps repeating. For just a moment she stops weeping when she sees Heather enter the room. "Heather, where's my baby?"

"Your baby? What baby? Susan? Are you talking about Susan? What's this about, Patricia? Why don't you know where Susan is?"

"Susan wasn't in her bed when Patricia woke up this morning," Gerald answers for his daughter. "I drove here from Elliot Lake as soon as I received Patricia's call early this morning. It's a long drive and I've been here for only half an hour. Since I got here I've been trying to calm her down but, as you can see, without any success. That's why I've called you, Heather. We need your help. You've got to do something."

"Oh, my God, Gerald. Where are the police? Have they started a search party yet?"

Without hesitation, Heather opens her medical bag, withdraws what is required and injects Patricia. Within moments Patricia is calm and soon sound asleep on the living-room couch.

"Gerald, I asked you have they started a search party yet? Why aren't the police here? Have they already left? I can't believe they would leave poor Patricia alone in the state she was in."

"The police haven't been here, Heather."

"What? Why on earth are they taking so long to get here? What time did you call them, Gerald?"

"I haven't called them yet, Heather. You're the only person I've called and to be quite frank I did not know what else to do."

"You didn't know what to do? Gerald, for heaven's sakes, call the police. Why haven't you called them? Call them right now! Have Susan's playmates been contacted? Could she have left the house and gone somewhere to play before Patricia woke up this morning?"

As he dialed the number for the police station, Gerald answers, "Patricia told me she did all that this morning before she called me." Then, "Yes, sir, I need to report a missing child."

Within ten minutes two police officers arrive at the door of Number Five Crabapple Court.

After questioning Heather the police allow her to return next door to her home. She walks back across her neighbour's front lawn to her own house. The first thing she does is to phone her husband, Ernie, at work. She explains the little she knows of the situation to him. "The police kept asking me why I put Patricia to sleep before they had their opportunity to question her. And they were right, Ernie. It was a stupid thing to do. I don't know why I did that."

"Calm down, Heather. Are the boys at home?"

"I don't even know. I haven't checked yet. I should get back to work but I'm so confused now. This whole situation has me extremely upset. I'm not sure what to do next."

"Heather, I'm with a client now but I'll do my best to cut things short here. I'm on my way home. Just stay there, put the kettle on, and by the time you have the tea made I'll be there, okay?"

"Yes," she says as she replaces the wireless phone into its pocket.

She makes her way into the large, sunny kitchen, fills the shiny metal kettle with water and turns on the stove's burner. "William! Harold! Is anybody home?" she shouts. "Gordon!"

"We're downstairs in the family room!" William yells back.

"Come upstairs, boys! I need to talk to you."

"We're in the middle of a game of darts, Mom. Be there in a second," Harold shouts back.

"Now! I want all three of you up here now! On the double!"

The kettle whistles. Heather withdraws three teabags from the canister on the counter, places them into the teapot before pouring in the bubbling water. She places the teapot onto the kitchen table, grabs five cups and saucers out of the cupboard, and has them set around the table before the three boys bound upstairs.

"Sit to the table, boys!" she orders. "Your Dad will be here soon. We all need to talk."

"What's up, Mom?" fifteen year old Harold asks.

Just then Heather hears Ernie's car pull into the driveway. "Your Dad's home now. Wait until he gets into the house, Harold." She pours tea into the five cups and then sits at the table awaiting her husband's arrival.

Ernie removes his suit jacket as he enters the kitchen and slings it over the back of a kitchen chair before he sits down at the table with his family. "Okay, we're all here, Heather. What's going on?"

"Susan's gone missing."

Thirteen year old Gordon asks, "You mean the little brat next door?"

"Gordon!"

"Sorry, Mom, but she is a little brat, always coming around and wanting me to play with her. I'm a teenager now for Pete's sake. I told her I don't play with seven year old kids but still she keeps bugging me and coming around wanting me to play."

"When did you last see her, Gordie?" his father asks.

Gordon thinks for just a minute before replying. "Yesterday afternoon. She was here for just a little while before I sent her packing. I told her to go play with kids her own age."

"Oh, she isn't such a bad kid, Gordie. I think she must be lonely. Can't be too easy being an only child with no father," William says. "I always feel a bit sorry for her."

"She had her grandfather," fifteen year old Harold offers.

That's when Gordon says, "She wasn't too crazy about her grandfather."

"What do you mean? How do you know that, Gordie?" his father asks.

"I know that because Susie told me that."

Heather spoke up, "What else did Susie have to say about her grandfather, Gordon?"

"That's all, just that the old guy is kind of weird."

"Susie said her grandfather is weird?" Heather asks.

"Yes."

"That's a strange thing to say if you ask me," Ernie says.

Heather shoots a warning look at her husband and then allows her eyes to wander from the face of one boy to the face of another. She loves her three sons but she knows they are not always the angels she would have liked them to be. Knowing it is just a matter of time before they will all be questioned by the police she feels she has to ask the question, "Do any of you have any idea what could have happened to Susie or any idea where Susan could be?"

"I told you, Mom, I haven't seen her since yesterday afternoon," Gordon repeats.

"And you, William?"

"I haven't seen the kid in a long while, Mom. I never paid much attention to her."

"Me neither," adds Harold.

"Your Mom is right, boys. The police will come here to question all of us. Is there anything; anything at all you know about the disappearance of Susie?"

"No, Dad, nothing."

"Are you okay, Heather?" Ernie asks.

"I'm mad at myself, Ernie. I never should have sedated Patricia and put her to sleep before she had a chance to talk to the police. I didn't even think twice about what I was doing. I could have used a lighter form of sedation without putting her out. It was really stupid of me to do what I did."

"Don't beat yourself up, Heather. You did what you thought was right at the time. Let it go. What's done is done. When the police get here I just want everybody to relax. Boys, just be sure to speak the truth and the questioning will soon be over."

***

It isn't until early the following day that the doorbell rings. Peering through the living room window Heather can see a tall man in a grey suit standing near the front door. Though not in uniform she thinks he looks like a cop. Ernie and the boys are out with the search party. She is home alone. He looks like a cop, she thinks, but what if he isn't? Feeling totally on edge she doesn't know whether to answer the door or not.

The doorbell rings again.

FIVE

FIVE:

#5 – *The Donnelly Family*

Matthew Donnelly is an award-winning architect. He has designed shopping centres, hotels and homes throughout major cities in Canada. In spite of his well-known fame and success, his favourite achievement is the house he designed for himself; a house in the style of Queen Anne. He loves the house in which he lives with his family at Number Five Crabapple Court in the small Town of Fairmont.

He moved into this house nine years ago with his wife, Doctor Patricia Donnelly. Patricia is a medical doctor, a general practitioner, who very quickly built up a private practice in Fairmont. She also works on call in the town's only hospital.

Two years into the marriage Patricia gives birth to a little girl. It is with pride that they name her Susan, after the baby's maternal grandmother, Patricia's mother, who died when Patricia was just a child.

Growing up without a mother had been a difficult challenge for Patricia and this gives her all the more reason to be delighted that her first child is a girl. She makes a secret promise to herself to be the best mother and best friend the little one could ever hope for.

Patricia had been raised primarily by her father, Gerald Gagnon. Although he hired nannies or baby-sitters while he worked in the mines, Gerald was her caregiver when he was at home which was much of the time. Growing up in the bustling mining town of Elliot Lake, Ontario, Patricia was often lonesome. She missed her mother.

Her father owns a hunting cabin not too far from his house in the City of Elliot Lake. The cabin is on a piece of lakefront land that offers a small beach where Patricia enjoyed her childhood summer weekends and vacation times when her father wasn't working.

Her father still owns the cabin to this day and now Patricia thinks of times in the future when she will take her little girl, Susan, out to the lake to play just as she, herself, had done throughout her lonely childhood.

When Susan is just three years old what happens turns Patricia's life upside down. Matthew becomes extremely ill with lung cancer. He suffers greatly in his final year and dies at the too early age of thirty-seven.

Devastated by this, the second major loss in her short life, Patricia puts her own needs on the back burner and proceeds to carefully divide her time between caring for her daughter and caring for her patients. Too often she hears herself repeating aloud the words, *Physician, heal thyself.*

Although she knows many people, Patricia has few close friends. She is grateful for the friendship of her next-door neighbour, Heather Martin, who is also a physician. She and Heather are co-workers at the Fairmont General Hospital.

After her husband's death Patricia does her best for Susan as a single mom. For five years, though she receives several invitations, she chooses not to date. She hires Nan Barton, an older woman in her sixties; a woman with a kind face and several grandchildren of her own, as baby-sitter for little Susan while she works at the hospital throughout each week.

Her father, Gerald, who is by now retired but still living in Elliot Lake, makes frequents visits to Fairmont. During these times he looks after Susie while Patricia works. This saves Patricia some money but much more important than the financial savings she appreciates that her daughter, Susie, has the influence of a man around the house during her father's visits.

From what Patricia can see the two get along very well together. Gerald spends time with Susan; reading to her; playing baseball and he has even taken her on a couple of fishing trips with the promise that he will take her on more once she is a little older.

But on more than one occasion Susan has come to her mother to complain. "I don't want to be with Grandad," she says.

"Why not, Susan?"

But Susan never provides a satisfactory answer. Instead she will just change the subject or run out of the house to play, ignoring her mother's question.

Perhaps because of her grandfather's influence, Susan is a bit of a tom-boy. She likes to go next door to the Martin household and play with thirteen-year-old Gordon. Often Susan will come home crying, "Gordon is mean. He won't play with me."

"You need to play with little girls who are closer to your own age, Susie," her mother suggests.

But Susan is bound and determined to play with Gordon. Again and again she comes home crying.

This particular morning Patricia awakens to the robins singing outside her bedroom window. It is a work day so she makes her way to the kitchen, tapping on Susan's bedroom door as she passes it. "Wake up, Susie."

In the kitchen she puts on the coffee then sets out the plates and bowls for Susan's usual breakfast of cereal and toast before dropping the bread slices into the toaster. Two small glasses she fills with orange juice and still, Susan has not come into the kitchen.

"Are you up, Susan?" Patricia shouts while she butters the toast and puts the slices onto the plates. "Come on now, breakfast is ready!"

When Susan still does not enter the kitchen, Patricia is very surprised but also extremely annoyed. If they don't soon get a move on she will be late for work and it was her morning to be on call at the hospital. She leaves the kitchen and goes to Susan's room. Upon opening the bedroom door, she is taken aback to see her child's bed rumpled but empty.

"Susie," she calls, "where are you? This is no time for games you little imp! Where are you hiding?"

Patricia looks under the bed, checks the three bathrooms in the house and then goes downstairs to see if she is playing a video game in the family room. There is no sign of Susie anywhere.

Nothing like this has ever happened before but Patricia tries to remain calm. She doesn't want to panic. Thinking Susie has probably gone next door to bother Gordon again she leaves the house, crosses the lawn to the neighbour's home and knocks on the door. The oldest boy, William, answers the door. "No, I haven't seen Susie this morning," he says before he calls out to his brothers, "Have either of you seen Susan Donnelly this morning?"

"Nope," both Harold and Gordon shout.

"Is your Mom home?" Patricia asks.

"She's already gone off to work," William answers. "Is anything wrong?"

"Well, it's just that Susie has never wandered off like this in the morning before. It's unusual but she is probably playing at a friend's house. I'll find her. Not to worry."

Patricia leaves Number Three Crabapple Court and walks out onto the street's interlock brick sidewalk. She isn't in the right mood to appreciate the fragrance of the crabapple blossoms as she journeys toward Number Nine, the home of George and Marian Cavendish who have an eight-year-old son named Robert. Sometimes Susan plays with Robert and Patricia hopes that maybe that is where she is hiding.

George Cavendish answers the door when Patricia rings the bell.

"No, I haven't seen Susie."

But before he closes the door he checks with his wife, Marian, and all three of his children to be certain no one in the family knows of Susan's whereabouts.

By now Patricia is beginning to panic. Yes, she knows that Susie has other friends from elementary school but she doesn't know every address or phone number. She feels very alone and frightened. As soon as she gets home she shouts, "Susie, where are you hiding?" She scours the house. She searches every room in it from top to bottom. She even looks inside the closets and cupboards wondering as she does, why she is doing so.

She calls the hospital and tells them she won't be in to work this day and then she calls the only person she knows who she believes can take care of everything. She phones her father, Gerald Gagnon.

He doesn't answer his home phone but she reaches him on his cell phone. He is spending some time at his hunting cabin out on the lake not far from the City of Elliot Lake.

"I'm on my way," he promises but it's going to take me a few hours to get there."

While awaiting the arrival of her father Patricia phones Susie's baby-sitter. "Hello, Nan. Is there any chance that Susie has shown up at your doorstep this morning?"

Surprised by the question, Nan Barton replies, "No, ma'am. Susie has never come by my house. Are you sure she's not over at her school?"

"At school? Nan, I didn't think of checking the school. Why would she go there? She knows there is no school in the summer."

"Yes, I know ma'am, but sometimes the kids like to play in the school yard."

"Thanks Nan. I'm going to check the school yard now."

Patricia begins to make the rounds of all the residential streets in town enquiring at the homes where Susan knows the children in the family. Then she visits the school yard. She also scans the beaches, the parks, and all the playgrounds. She searches for hours with no success.

Upon arriving home, she collapses on the couch. That's where she is when her father arrives. He finds her on the couch, hugging a pillow, hysterical and crying, *Baby, where are you, baby?*

By the time Gerald arrives at his daughter's home it is past two p.m. in the afternoon. He tries to calm Patricia down but meets with no success.

Not knowing what else to do, he calls Heather. If he knows nothing else, he knows his daughter needs medical help. "Heather, you must come quickly."

Heather arrives and sedates Patricia. Then she asks, "Where are the police? What time did you call them?"

Gerald confesses he has not called them yet. "I'll call them now," he says and that's exactly what he does.

When the two officers arrive they question Gerald. "When is the last time you saw your grand-daughter, sir?"

"That was weeks ago. I don't live here in Fairmont. I just arrived a short while ago from my hunting cabin in Elliot Lake. I know nothing of Susan's disappearance other than what my daughter has told me. She has searched everywhere and cannot find her."

The police also question Heather. "We want to know why you sedated Doctor Donnelly to such a degree before we had a chance to talk with her."

Heather struggles to come up with a satisfactory response.

Heavily sedated, Patricia does not awaken for another two hours. This is when the police begin their questioning of her.

She answers their questions and gives them a recent photo of her daughter. "This is Susie," she says. "Please find my little girl."

"Yes, ma'am. We will do our best," Chief Morris promises.

"We're on it," Officer Taylor states.

SIX

SIX:

#7 – *The Kovacs Family*

Daniel Kovacs and his wife Marsha live in a unique, white Georgian home that boasts a centre hall plan which is the envy of all who visit. The house has fabulous curb appeal with its striking black shutters and manicured lawn and garden. Anyone admiring the house from the boardwalk on the other side of the street imagines how wonderful it must be to live in such a place; how very fortunate the inhabitants are to enjoy such an extravagant lifestyle.

Indeed Daniel, who is one of the two dentists residing and working in the Town of Fairmont, does enjoy his affluent lifestyle. He is very happy and content with his lot in life. He works hard and his hours are long but, yes, the rewards are great. Not for one minute does he regret his decision to move away from the prosperous practice he had prior enjoyed in Toronto to the small suburban Town of Fairmont. He had grown tired of the city's never ending noise and bustle and has learned to appreciate the peace and quiet that small town living offers.

His wife, Marsha, does not share Daniel's feelings of gratitude. In the large Toronto metropolis she had enjoyed a busy psychotherapy practice. She had even returned to college to develop her own sense of spirituality; her own desire for wholeness, a desire that was never quite achieved. Her additional college credits allowed her to change her professional title from Psychotherapist to that of Psychospiritual Practitioner. In Toronto she worked with many, mostly female, clients who were experiencing relationship problems.

Their move to the beautiful suburban home in Fairmont has a negative effect on Marsha's career. She soon discovers that in this small town there are few women who are willing to seek help with their relationship issues, though they are many. She has even been told by some, over the phone of course in order to protect their own identity and privacy, that they would love to be able to come to her for advice and counsel but that they can't because they are much too prominent and well-known in the Town of Fairmont. It would never do to get around that they were seeing a psychotherapist.

This narrow view of her profession is very upsetting to Marsha. In Toronto clients brag about their therapists and they are proud of the fact that they are on what they term "paths of self-discovery". This is a far cry from the shame and embarrassment with which Fairmont's small town residents view the possibility of asking for help.

And, of course, Marsha needs to take into account the fact that the majority of the women in this working-class small town do not have the financial means in order to afford the services that she is qualified to offer.

For these reasons Marsha's client base changes dramatically from what it had been in Toronto. Now the vast majority of the people who come to her for help are unwilling clients sent to her by agencies such as the Welfare Department, the Drug and Alcohol Rehabilitation Centre or Prison officials. These clients do nothing to diminish the importance of her work; in fact they have the opposite impact. However in this process Marsha is losing sight of her own spiritual goals. She sometimes falls into depression.

She very much wants a child; someone of her very own to love and care for; someone who will love her in return. But it is not to be. It is not for lack of trying but Marsha has never yet succeeded in getting pregnant.

More than once over the years she has approached her husband, Daniel, about the possibility of adopting a child. Without ever giving her a satisfactory reason for his refusal, he simply tells her he will not consider adopting a child.

The childless Marsha has now reached the age of forty-two. She attends the Methodist Church that is right at the corner of her street and it is there that she sings in the choir.

She has no housekeeper and just keeping her beautiful large home clean and tidy takes up most of her free time. She also does the cooking for their main meal of each day. These tasks combined with her therapy practice keep her busy but none of these tasks serve to make her feel fulfilled and happy. None of these activities fill the emptiness; the hole that sometimes drives her to despair; the black hole that too often she falls into where she experiences the pain stored within the dark depths of her soul.

Marsha wants a child. She needs a child. It is not easy for her to accept that these needs will not be met.

She is home alone that afternoon when she answers the door to find two police officers standing on her doorstep. Upon seeing their uniforms she feels faint and dizzy. Without warning she passes out on the foyer floor. One of the officers stays with her while the other calls her husband who is at work in his dental office.

"Please come on home, Mr. Kovacs," the officer requests. "Your wife is unwell and needs you here. And in addition we have questions for both of you. It will help us considerably if we can question you together."

"I'm on my way," the puzzled Daniel replies.

He arrives home within five minutes. Even though their phone call had alerted him it still seems quite shocking to him to see a police car parked in his driveway.

The questioning soon begins.

SEVEN

SEVEN:

#9 – The Cavendish Family

Even by the occupants of its neighbours the house located at Number Nine Crabapple Court is termed an odd looking place. It is formidable and known to have been given several renovations. There are three additions made to what was originally a pretty ranch style bungalow.

Number Nine is owned by George Cavendish who is even more formidable and perhaps even more odd in appearance than his home given the fact that he is only five feet two and a half inches tall but carries a weight of more than two hundred pounds. He cares nothing for fashion and on most days he can be seen wearing blue jeans with a plaid shirt which makes a hapless attempt to hide the pot belly that has nowhere to hang but over his belt. His head is balding and it is rare that he is spotted around town without a lit Cuban cigar dangling from his lips.

George Cavendish is a wealthy man. He literally owns the one-industry town called Fairmont because that one industry just happens to be the Cavendish Paper Mill where the majority of Fairmont residents work. He also owns the local hotel, the movie theatre and more than half the buildings situated along Main Street.

His philosophy concerning women is a simple one. "Keep 'em barefoot and pregnant," is his favourite motto and one that he puts into practice.

His wife Marian is a housewife. If anyone asks her why she doesn't have a professional career she answers, "I've got a full time job just putting up with George." And she will not be joking when she answers in that fashion. In her opinion George is not an easy man to live with.

Together they have three children. Their youngest is eight-year-old Robert who is a playmate of Susan Donnelly. At this early age Robert has already failed a grade and he will soon share a classroom with Susie. In the fall they will both be attending grade two in the local elementary school.

Dolores is next in line; a clever sixteen year old who attends grade eleven. She is a vivacious cheerleader and looks forward to returning to school once September rolls around.

Last but certainly not to be ignored is the first child born to Marian and George. Marian dubs him a handful and George, a pain in the neck throughout his growing-up years. Thomas, at nineteen, is already known to the local police for his rowdiness, vandalism and downright drunkenness. His favourite hang-out is the local pool hall and it is said that he is making money on the side by not just smoking, but also selling those funny, strange smelling cigarettes. And more recently it is said that Thomas is spending time hanging around the playground at the town's elementary school. No one is sure why but the police have their suspicions.

Marian worries about Thomas while George simply whacks him upside the head and says, "You're acting like a low-life! Smarten up!"

The last time the police knocked on the door of number nine Crabapple Court was to question Thomas about his newly acquired habit of hanging around the playground at the local elementary school. Not for the first time he is suspected of selling drugs to the youngsters but so far no proof has been discovered nor have there been any charges laid against him.

"I aint selling no drugs to no little kids," Thomas insists. "I wouldn't do a thing like that. Why, I like kids; I like kids a lot."

That morning when Patricia Donnelly comes knocking on the door of Number Nine, Marian calls her young son, Robert, to the door.

"I can't find Susie, Robert. Do you know where she is? Have you seen her today?" Patricia asks.

"Nope," Robert replies. "I saw her yesterday but I haven't seen her today. I haven't even been outside to play yet today."

"It's the truth he's telling you, Patricia," Marian states. "He hasn't gone outside to play yet today."

"You haven't seen my Susie, Marian?"

"No, I'm sorry to tell you I have not. I hope you can find her soon. Kids sure can be a worry at times."

"Why did Susie run away?" young Robert asks his mother after Patricia departs.

"Why on earth would a little girl run away from such a lovely family?" Marian answers.

The next time Marian's doorbell rings that day she opens the door to see two uniformed police officers standing tall right there in front of her. She wonders what Thomas has been up to this time.

"We have a few questions for you and your family members, ma'am. Is everyone at home?"

"Yes, everyone but my husband, George. He'll be here soon enough though. It's almost supper time.

"If you don't mind, ma'am, we will just sit out here on the porch step until your husband returns. We would like to have you all present when we ask our questions."

"Suit yourself, boys," Marian replies. "Suit yourself."

EIGHT

EIGHT:

The Colletti Family

The impressive colonial revival home with its large white pillars over the massive front entrance is Number Eleven Crabapple Court; the home of the Colletti Family. Like his neighbours on the same street Mario Colletti is a wealthy man. At sixty-five years of age he is much older than the occupants of the few exclusive homes that share his street. His two daughters are adults now living in Toronto.

Once they had graduated from college they couldn't wait to move away from home and away from their father's tightwad practices. It is his very stinginess that motivated both daughters to advance well and quickly in their own careers. Never again, they vowed, will they depend financially upon their father or any man for that matter.

Both girls marry well and in a few short years Mario becomes a grandfather but he keeps himself busy as an investment banker. He is definitely not what one would describe as a family man. In fact he spends little time with his wife and daughters. He rarely sees his grandchildren and that is fine with him. It is his opinion that he has better things to do with his time and with his money.

Mario's wife lives her life in strict contrast to that of her husband. In the early days prior to their marriage, when Annette clerks in the department store where Mario shops for his inexpensive shirts and ties, she is a quiet girl. She is said to have told her family members that she is a little in awe of Mario's position and the wealth that results from his labour.

Annette's father was a sanitation worker for the Town of Fairmont. Before his retirement he spent his working days picking up garbage and driving it to the Town Site Dump. This is work he does for years until the day he turns sixty-five and can finally retire on his old-age government pension.

Throughout her life Annette's mother never works outside the home but while she spends her time taking care of Annette and her two siblings, she also sells Avon products to other housewives. Following the tradition her mother had started, Annette also sells Avon products to neighbouring women. She doesn't need to earn money but she is a sociable woman and enjoys staying in touch with the local women. These housewives, unlike herself, carry mortgages or they pay monthly rents for the small, modest homes in which they live in the Town of Fairmont. Their husbands are clerks in the hardware store, sanitation workers for the town as her father had been or mill hands who complain about the shift work they do from one year to the next.

Accustomed as she is to her parents' working class lifestyle Annette is very much at home in the homes of these women many of whom were her childhood playmates. And because of her background it is not surprising to anyone that upon her marriage to Mario, she tackles the challenge of maintaining what, to her, is his mansion on Crabapple Court.

"It's a lot of hard, physical work, Mom," she exclaims. "We could fit half your house into his foyer."

Annette awakens early each day, works hard and meets the daunting challenge. She not only keeps his house clean, she raises his children and seldom asks him for a penny to visit the stylist to get her hair done or to relax with a manicure or a pedicure at the spa. These activities are not part of her experience but she knows that these are simple things that the other women on Crabapple Court take for granted as an ordinary part of their everyday lifestyle.

Although married to a wealthy man and living in a luxurious home, Annette slugs away and works harder than any working class housewife. She asks for next to nothing for herself.

And this is exactly how Mario likes her to be. This is exactly why he chose her to be his wife. He doesn't want a woman who will be high maintenance. No, he wants to spend as little as possible and keep a tight control on his hard-earned money.

It isn't until Annette's daughters grow up and leave the family home to reside in Toronto that she begins to see the folly of her ways. Because both girls have achieved solid well-paying careers and because they married well to men who also earned high incomes, Annette is able to observe how women of wealth can and, indeed, should enjoy life.

It is common knowledge and everyone in Fairmont knows to whom Annette is married. Encouraged by her daughters she applies for and receives both a Visa card and a MasterCard. It doesn't take her long to catch on to the simplicity of paying for purchases with these magical cards.

And when the grandchildren start to come along, Annette develops a brand new passion. She discovers that she loves to shop for them; something she never did for her own children. She buys lots of popular toys and expensive clothing. She loves to visit Toronto where she baby-sits the children. She loves to take them to the museums, the art galleries, the amusement parks and the zoo. And as the grandchildren grow older she continues to spoil them by buying them designer fashion, the latest in computer games and virtually anything they ask for.

Because she has grown so very busy spending time with her grandchildren, Annette discovers that she is no longer able to fit the humdrum housework, laundry and grocery shopping into her weekly schedule.

While Mario complains about her extravagant spending, Annette closes her ears and refuses to listen to him. She does not discuss with him the necessity of a housekeeper. She simply hires Annie Benjamin to do all the chores that had at one time kept her tied to her husband and to his house.

Annie Benjamin is a good housekeeper. But she is also a good woman who makes unfortunate choices when it comes to choosing a boyfriend. It is not uncommon for Annie to arrive for work at Annette's kitchen door with a black eye, a bruised arm or a scratched face. Annie's boyfriend, Ronald, has a mean streak wider than the front lawn and deeper than the backyard swimming pool that no one uses anymore now that the girls are grown and gone from home.

Annie confides in Annette. "He's a mean man and I don't know how to keep him off me. But what worries me the most is the way he eyes my little girl, Arabella. If he ever lays a hand on my Arabella I swear I'll kill him."

"Has he ever hurt your little girl, Annie?"

"No ma'am, not that I know of and he better not! Maybe I shouldn't tell you this, Ms. Colletti, but I've heard rumors that a few years ago my Ronald messed around with a little girl in the Toronto projects. He did things with that child no grown man is supposed to do. I don't even know if the rumors are true but just knowing someone thought he could do something like that scares me to death. He better not ever hurt my Arabella. He just better not, that's all!"

That afternoon when the doorbell rings Mario is upstairs in the house, at his desk, scowling and swearing at the number of what he terms unnecessary purchases that his wife has made that month. Annette is in the kitchen with Annie talking about what could be done to keep Ronald away from Arabella.

It is Annie who opens the door. She is surprised to see the two uniformed police officers standing there but when they ask to see Mr. Colletti she swallows her fear and invites them into the house.

NINE

NINE:

Kidnap

The two officers spend the entire afternoon and early evening speaking with the occupants of the five houses on Crabapple Court. Leaning back in his chair, the elder of the two, Officer Madison Morris, tosses his cap onto his desk, raises his long legs and rests his big feet atop the cluttered desk beside his hat. "What do you think, Nick?"

The younger officer, Nick Taylor, sits in the plain wooden chair across the desk from his boss and scratches his head. "Can't say for sure but looks like a kidnap to me, Maddy."

"Yep, doesn't look good, Nick. We've got ourselves a lot of suspects."

"It's hard to know where to begin, boss. Every house on Crabapple Court has at least one suspect living in it."

"Okay, let's run it down. Top of the list is Doctor Heather Martin. We've got to ask the question; why was she in such a big hurry to put the kid's mother to sleep? Does she know who has kidnapped the girl? Was she trying to protect someone; trying to give him more time to get away? What about those big sons of hers? We've got a long list of questions for those boys."

"Yes, boss, and on that list let's not forget the girl's grandfather, Gerald Gagnon. We've already heard that the kid thinks her grandfather is weird and she doesn't like to be with him."

"No, Nick, I'm pretty sure the old man is clear. He was up in Elliot Lake, miles away from the crime scene. No, I think we can knock him off the list of suspects."

"Well, okay, boss, if you say so. What about that Marsha Kovacs? No kids of her own and who is to say she wouldn't kidnap someone else's kid to satisfy her own needs to be a mother? I once saw a movie about a woman who kidnapped for that very reason."

"Hmm, never thought of that one, Nick, but, yes, though I think it is unlikely let's keep her on our list for now. I'm more inclined to wonder about her psychotherapy clients. She has guys from the rehab centre and the ex-cons coming to her house. I think we need to get a full list of her clients and check them all out."

"Yep, that might be easier said than done, boss, but we will give it a shot. There's also Thomas Cavendish; as if we didn't already know too much about that guy!"

"It's true he's been hanging around the elementary school playground. Some say he's pushing drugs on the young kids but he denies it and we've got no proof. The missing girl is only seven; can't see that Tom would be selling drugs to a kid that young but then who knows these days, eh? We'll keep him on the list; have him in for further questioning."

"Okay, boss, and what about that boyfriend of Annie Benjamin? Annie is showing up for work with cuts and bruises. The guy is an obvious abuser."

"Nothing to tie him to Susie or the Donnelly family though, Nick."

"True again, boss. But seems to me Annie has a kid of her own not much different in age than this Donnelly girl. Just makes me kind of wonder, that's all."

"If you have a hunch we will follow it up, Nick. Now, let's see, how many do we have on the list so far?"

"Five houses; and at least five suspects, boss. Want to list them by address?"

"Why not? It's as good a way to go as any."

"Okay, Number Three Crabapple Court we have Dr. Heather Martin. Why was she so quick to inject the kid's mother and put her to sleep? Was she trying to keep her from talking to the police in an attempt to protect one of her own boys?"

"All right, Nick, and in Number Five Crabapple Court we have no suspects. That's where the kid is missing and nobody there but the mother and the kid's grandfather. No suspects."

"Okay, boss, if you say so. Then in Number Seven we have two suspects."

"List the two, Nick."

"Okay. Number one is Marsha Kovacs. No kids of her own and who is to say she didn't steal someone else's child? And number two suspect is one of Marsha Kovacs' crazy clients; an ex-con or a guy from the rehab centre."

"All right, Nick, and that takes us next to Number Nine Crabapple Court and that nineteen year old drunk, Thomas Cavendish. Let's find out why he's been hanging around that elementary school playground. I think there's a lot more to him than meets the eye."

"And in Number Eleven, boss, we've got the housekeeper's boyfriend, Ronald. We know he's an abuser but let's find out if he likes to abuse kids too."

"So how many suspects so far, Nick?"

"Five; we've got a good five to start with and who knows where that will lead."

"We will start calling them in to the station one by one." Glancing at his wrist watch he says, "It's really getting late. Let's call it a night and we will get an early start in the morning."

"I hate to think of where that little girl is spending this night, boss."

"It's a sick world we live in, Nick.

"You got that right, boss."

And in this way the two officers have scratched the surface of the initial investigation into the disappearance of the missing child, Susan Donnelly. They believe they are off to a good start. In the morning the real work will begin.

TEN

TEN:

Where is Susan Donnelly?

This is not an ordinary morning in The Town of Fairmont. It's a Sunday morning and with some exceptions the townspeople don't have to report to work. They listen to the radio; see reports on TV and many of them have already read the article in the local paper. Others can't wait to get out of the house to pick up the morning's paper. They don't need an invitation. A child is missing. That's all they need to know. They pull together and go straight into action.

With some still dressed in their pyjamas, nightgowns and bathrobes the residents of The Town of Fairmont greet each other on their postage stamp lawns as they head toward the ends of their driveways to pick up the local Sunday paper. The headline on this morning's Fairmont Times is no longer whispering. It is shouting with the best of them, *SEARCH FOR SUSAN STARTS THIS MORNING.*

"Are you going to be part of the search party?" one neighbour asks.

"Can't go; gotta stay home with the kids but my George is going, you bet! And my oldest boy Danny, he will be part of it too. Where are they gathering?"

"It's probably in this morning's paper but what I heard on TV is the search party is being organized on the boardwalk."

"Right across from the kid's house, eh?"

"Yep, that's what I heard but best you should read the paper in case I've got it wrong. Are you going to be part of the search party?"

"You bet I am! Poor kid!"

"Yeah, I'm scared to let mine outside the house; gotta keep 'em close by, you know?"

"Yeah, I know. Glad my kids are grown so I don't have to worry. I just hope they find the girl soon"

"Yeah, me too. Well, gotta go get dressed and I want to read this morning's paper."

"Yep, see ya later!"

Heather Martin sees the massive crowd of people gathering across the road on the boardwalk. There are so many people they are spilling onto the sandy beach. She hesitates to go outside to pick up her newspapers but she wants to know what is going on. Even though she lives right next door to the victim's family she doesn't know anything more than anyone else.

She knows Susie is missing since yesterday morning. She thinks of going next door to be with her fellow physician and friend, Patricia. How awful to lose a child. She can't imagine it and is grateful that her three boys are now all in their teen years and less likely to be the eye candy these kidnappers are looking for.

Yes, she thinks of going next door using the houses' back doors to be out of the gathering crowd's view but she decides against it. She knows Patricia is not alone. Her father, Gerald, is there to care for her and surely he will call her again if he needs her. She still has regrets about giving Patricia such a strong sedative but at the time she cared only to help her friend find some rest and peace. She is annoyed with herself because it didn't even occur to her that she should wait until after Patricia had talked to the police. With a sigh she has to accept that what is done can't be undone. There is no way I can change what has taken place, she thinks, as she makes her way down her own driveway to retrieve the morning papers.

With her frustration level at an all-time high she complains aloud to no one there, "Why can't these lazy kids deliver the papers to the door?" She can't believe what is before her eyes! Well, at least I'm dressed in my track suit and not in my bathrobe like a lot of the women on the boardwalk. I see some of them still have curlers in their hair. Good grief! Don't they care what they look like on TV?

Heather's thoughts are like jellybeans in a jar; too many of them and all piled one on top of the other. TV? Oh, my god, and here I am in my track suit. I should have dressed properly. Better yet I should have stayed in the house.

She has reached the end of her driveway and picked up from the grass at the foot of her lawn the three newspapers. She picks up all three but unfolds The Fairmont Times first. The headline reads *SEARCH FOR SUSAN STARTS THIS MORNING.*

That explains the massive gathering across the road, Heather realizes. She begins to make her way back up the driveway toward her house but in no time at all she is ganged up on and surrounded by TV cameras and noisy reporters.

"Mrs. Martin, will you answer some questions for us?"

Unsure what to do, Heather keeps walking toward her house. "I have no comments. I've just come out for my newspapers."

"Mrs. Martin, you gave Mrs. Donnelly the injection that put her to sleep. Why didn't you wait for the police to arrive before you did that?"

How do they know that? Heather quickens her pace. She can see TV cameras everywhere. She raises the three newspapers in front of her face to shield herself from the cameras. This is a bloody circus, she thinks, but she says no more to the reporters.

"Mrs. Martin, how long have you lived next door to the Donnelly family?" is the last question she hears before she gets back inside and closes the door on the aggressive, unrelenting reporters. *Pushy people!*

Back inside the house Heather leans her back on the door and calls her sons into the foyer. When they arrive she orders, "Stay in the house today. Under no circumstances are you to leave this house, do you hear me?"

"Mom, what's the matter with you? Why are you behaving this way?" William asks. "We all thought we could help. There's no good reason I can think of to prevent us from being a part of the search party."

Just then Ernie Martin comes into the foyer where his entire family is gathered. "What's going on?" he asks

"We want to be part of the search party," William answers.

"She's our next door neighbour, for Pete's sake. We should be helping," Harold shouts.

"Mom doesn't want us to go," thirteen year old Gordon complains.

Ernie looks at his wife. He can see she is visibly shaken.

"Heather? What's going on?" he repeats his question.

"They are forming a search party across the street on the boardwalk."

"That's good," Ernie says. "We can all be part of that search party if they want us there."

"The reporters," Heather cries.

"What about the reporters?"

"Ernie, I just went out for the papers. They swooped down on me like a pack of vultures. They all wanted to know why I gave Patricia such a heavy sedative. They acted like I'm a suspect for God's sake."

"Calm down, Heather," her husband reaches out and holds her in his arms until she is able to control her tears. "That's all the more reason why the boys and I need to get across the street and join that search party."

"Dad's right, Mom," William states.

"Yeah, Mom," Harold agrees.

"You've got to let us go, Mom," Gordon asserts.

With a heavy sigh Heather relents. "You will stay with the boys, Ernie?"

"Of course I will, Heather."

"And you boys stay with your Dad! That includes you, William. You all stay together, promise?"

"Yes, Mom," the three boys promise.

"You will all have some breakfast first. I want to see what's in the papers this morning."

The headline in the Toronto Star reads *DOCTOR DRUGS MOM BEFORE POLICE CAN QUESTION.*

Oh, my God, Ernie. No wonder the reporters are hounding me like that! She hands the newspaper to her husband. "How do they all know that anyway? Who told the reporters that I put Patricia to sleep before the police arrived? Only the local police knew that and surely they wouldn't give out that kind of information."

"Patricia's father knew, didn't he?"

"Well, yes, Ernie, but surely he wouldn't have told that to reporters, would he? I mean he's the one who was urging me to help Patricia. She was hysterical. They are making it look like I was trying to hide something."

"Try not to let all this get to you, Heather. Let me see the Globe. What's the headline there?"

Heather passes the Globe and Mail to her husband before resting her arms on the kitchen table and cradling her head in her arms.

RCMP CALLED IN – WHERE IS SUSAN DONNELLY? he read. RCMP? They must feel pretty sure it is a kidnapping then.

Heather lifts her head and asks, "What else could it be, Ernie?"

"Maybe Susie ran away." Gordon offers.

"Ran away?" Heather is yelling. "Why on earth would a pretty little thing like Susie run away from a good, loving home? That makes no sense, Gordon."

The search party is forming across the street on the boardwalk. Officers Madison Morris and Nick Taylor are doing their best to organize the crowd. Their plan was to start calling in suspects for questioning this morning but what with all the TV and newspaper coverage this kidnapping case is getting to be more than they can handle. Chief Morris contacted the RCMP and they are already on the job.

"It's a good turnout, Maddy," Officer Taylor observes.

"Yep, this boardwalk is a good central point to start. Let's get all these folks to form eight separate groups. We will give each group a direction and area where they can go to commence their search."

"Sounds good, Maddy."

And so the search party groups are formed and each group is assigned an area to cover. Ernie and the Martin boys stay together with one larger group keeping their promise to Heather.

Officers Morris and Taylor are more interested in noticing who does not show up for the search party than they are in those who do arrive.

"I see her family here but no sign of Doctor Martin," Chief Morris says.

"Yep, and no sign of the girl's grandfather either."

"No, Nick, but his daughter needs him. I wouldn't expect him to show up. No, the old man is in the clear. But I don't see any sign of that Tom Cavendish either."

"It's not likely he'd show up anywhere that police are involved, Maddy. There is no way he's going to help us out."

"I still think that kid is a likely suspect. But there is no sign of Annie Benjamin's boyfriend, Ronald, either."

"Yep, Maddy, it's a puzzle. Guess it's a good job the RCMP is taking on the investigation. It's too much for just you and me, boss."

"They may have counted us out, Nick, but I'm not counting myself out. Let the RCMP do their thing. I've got some ideas of my own."

"Sure boss, I'm with you." Officer Nick Taylor looks around and when he looks in the direction of the Donnelly house he says, "Well, for the love of Pete, would you look at that, boss?"

Chief Morris turns to look where Nick is pointing. "Now that's a nice thing to do, Nick, don't you think?"

The officers are watching as Fairmont residents in a very orderly fashion leave the boardwalk and cross the road to stand on the interlock brick sidewalk in front of the Donnelly home. When there are too many to occupy the sidewalk they gather between the blossoming Crabapple trees on the grassy boulevard.

The officers can see that the people are carrying objects in their hands; some have glass jars containing candles; some carry bouquets of flowers while others have pieces of paper, cards or cardboard where they have written their caring sentiments. It is obvious that they are creating a memorial for the missing child.

"Do they think the kid is dead, Maddy?"

"I don't know, Nick. There's no evidence to say the kid is dead. I think they are just wanting the family to know that they care about little Susie, that's all. Nobody thinks the kid is dead."

"I hope she's not, Maddy."

Just a little way down the street from the memorial garden the Jesus freaks are gathering. Carrying signs that scream *Jesus is the only way* and *Seek ye first the kingdom of God* they form a large circle beneath the crabapple trees on the boulevard. Holding hands they all start praying aloud and soon they are all singing *Amazing Grace, how sweet the sound to save a wretch like me; I once was lost but now I'm found ……..*

TV reporters for CTV and CBC hover here, there and everywhere. Everything will be on the six o'clock news.

"It's turning into a bloody circus!" Chief Morris says to his partner.

"We may need to call in some help, Maddy. Things could get out of hand."

"Yep, already done that. The OPP will be here soon, Nick. I put in a request a while ago. We need some help with crowd control just to keep order. We don't want things to get out of hand. Look, Nick, the search parties are leaving the area now. This is good. It will be easier to control the crowd now that many people are leaving the area."

"Hope they find the girl, boss."

"I almost hope they don't, Nick. But, if they do, I hope they find her alive. By the way, Nick, here are the keys to the police car. I'm going to be driving my own green Chevy for a while."

"You are?" Nick asks. "What's that about boss?"

"Just following a hunch, Nick. Just following a hunch," he says with a surreptitious smile.

ELEVEN

ELEVEN:

Thomas Cavendish

Visibly shaken, Tom Cavendish makes his way to the back of his house. Hoping he would not be seen he enters the back door and makes his way up the back stairway to his room.

He felt sick to his stomach. He hadn't meant to do it.

She had been watching him as he slipped the drugs to the older kids and then slipped their bills into his jeans pockets.

"I want some candy too, Tom," Susan begs.

Tom wishes the kid's mother would keep a closer eye on this kid. Susan Donnelly had been coming every morning for close to a week now. When she begged for candy Tom had been giving her a Pez from a packet he usually kept in the pocket of his blue jeans just to shut her up. But this morning he didn't have any Pez. He had nothing but prescription drugs and he wasn't about to start pushing to a kid as young as Susie.

"Get lost kid!"

"How come I can't have some, Tom? Do you want I should get you some money too like the big kids? Maybe Mommy will give me some money."

"Get lost I said! Beat it kid!"

"You are a meanie, Tom! I want some candy too. I see you give it to all the other kids."

Oh, my God! If this kid ever decides to tell anyone about this he will need to leave town in a big hurry. Thomas Cavendish was annoyed; more than annoyed he was afraid. His eyes wandered in all directions. He didn't want to be spotted talking to a kid so small. "How old are you anyway kid?"

"I'm seven."

"Well, you're too young! Beat it!"

Susan stood her ground. "I'm not scared of you Tom Cavendish! I want candy! If you don't give me some I'm going to tell my Mommy how mean you are to me."

"No, kid, don't do that."

"I will so!"

"I can't give you any candy today, Susan. The ones I have are just for big kids."

"I'm big enough!"

"You're not. Now scram! Beat it kid!"

TWELVE

TWELVE:

RCMP - #5 Crabapple Court

Gerald Gagnon stands at the living room window of Number Five Crabapple Court. At the sidewalk edge of the front lawn he can see a bunch of people piling up a lot of stuff. "It looks like cards and candles and who knows what else," he says to his daughter, Patricia.

"Why are they doing that, Dad? Do they think my baby is dead?"

"No, Patricia. Don't think things like that. I'm sure it's just their way of letting you know you are not alone."

"I am alone, Dad. Nobody can know how I'm feeling. I heard on the news they are forming search parties."

"It's kind of hard to see past the Crabapple trees but I can see there is a big bunch of people on the boardwalk. Maybe they are getting the search parties together there."

"We should be in a search party, Dad."

"No, Patricia. We will stay right where we are. You need to be by the phone."

"Dad, don't you think it's strange that I haven't heard anything from the kidnappers? I mean there's been no ransom note, no call to tell me where to take the money or anything like that."

"I don't know, Patricia. I don't know what's considered usual in cases like this."

Patricia, still wearing the same clothes she had on the day before, is sitting in an armchair in her living room. She has slept off and on in this chair overnight but there is no rest to be found for her. She hasn't combed her hair, nor has she showered or applied any make-up. Her slacks and sleeveless summer blouse are rumpled and disheveled.

Her father, Gerald Gagnon, on the other hand, had gone into the guest room around midnight. He had the opportunity to sleep throughout the night. This morning he is freshly shaven, wearing a clean shirt and for a man who is said to love his grand-daughter, he is showing little emotion. He appears quite calm and collected.

"I'll make you some breakfast, Patricia," he offers.

"I'm not hungry, Dad."

"Then just a little tea and toast," he insists. "You have to eat something, Patricia. You need to keep your strength up."

Ignoring her protest he goes into the kitchen.

Patricia jumps when the loud ring shrieks beside her. She picks up the phone on its first ring. "Hello."

"Mrs. Donnelly, it's me, Nan Barton. How can I help you, dear? Would you like me to come over to your house?"

"No, Nan. There is no need."

"I just can't understand how Susie could disappear like this, Patricia. I've been your baby-sitter long enough to know she is a good little girl. I don't think she wouldn't just up and wander off on her own."

"This is not a good time for me to talk to you, Nan. I need to keep the phone line open for the police and for, well, I just need to keep the line open, you understand."

"Yes, Patricia. God bless you. If you are sure you don't need me then I will join the search party. We will find her, Patricia. We will find our little Susie. I am keeping you in my prayers."

"Thank you, Nan."

Within moments after the phone call, the doorbell demands that Patricia get up from her chair to answer the door. First of all she walks to the living-room window. Peering out she can see there are two people standing there on the doorstep; a man and a woman. She doesn't recognize either of them; has no idea who they are. *Are they the kidnappers*?

The doorbell rings again. This time the bell brings Gerald back into the living-room from the kitchen. "Who is it, Patricia? Can you see who it is?"

"I don't know who they are, Dad. It's a man and a woman."

Gerald crosses the room and stands by his daughter. "They look like they might be cops," he says.

"They're not cops, Dad. I know the local police officers, Madison and Nick. These two are strangers. I've never seen these people before."

The doorbell sounds again.

"You sit down, Patricia. I'll get the door."

Patricia returns to her chair. Tucking her legs up under her she attempts to curl herself into as small a ball as she can manage. From the living-room she can hear her father's voice as he speaks to the strangers.

"Who are you? What do you want?" he asks.

Showing Gerald their badges the man and woman introduce themselves.

"I am RCMP Inspector Raymond Fletcher and this is Officer Margaret Owens. May we come in, sir?"

They are both dressed in ordinary street clothes. Gerald notices that the woman is carrying a very large black suitcase of some sort.

Gerald opens the door wider. "Yes, come in please. My daughter is in the living-room."

Inspector Fletcher and Officer Owens make their way into the living-room. They introduce themselves to Patricia. "Please make yourselves comfortable on the sofa," she offers. "Have you found my little girl yet?"

"Not yet, ma'am," Officer Owens responds. "But the search has begun and other members of our investigative team are hard at work, I can assure you. Are you able to answer a few questions for us, ma'am?"

"Yes, but this is all a nightmare. I mean nothing unusual happened. I woke up as usual and I thought Susie was sleeping. I knocked on her bedroom door as always and called out to her to wake up. I started preparing breakfast and when Susan didn't come into the kitchen I went into her room to hurry her up. I was shocked to see that her bed was empty."

Officer Owen looks up from his notebook and addresses Gerald who is standing, listening, in the doorway of the living-room. "Who are you, sir?"

"My name is Gerald Gagnon. I am Patricia's father and Susan's grandfather."

"Sir, it is understandable that your daughter is very distraught. Is there anyone else in the house? A housekeeper perhaps?"

"No," Gerald replies. "There is no one here except my daughter and me."

"In that case then, sir," Inspector Fletcher continued, "will you be so kind as to make a pot of hot tea. A cup of tea will do wonders for your daughter and I could do with a cup myself."

Surprised by the request, Gerald replies, "I was just in the kitchen when you came to the door. I was making some breakfast for my daughter; just a little tea and toast. Would you also like some toast with your tea."

"Thank you, that is very kind of you."

With that Gerald leaves the living-room. Officer Owens softly speaks to Patricia. "We just wanted him out of the room. We wanted to be alone with you, Mrs. Donnelly. I hope your father won't mind making a little extra toast this morning."

"Mrs. Donnelly," Inspector Fletcher asks, "Do you have a photo of your daughter?"

"Yes, I have many," Patricia says. "I already gave one to Chief Morris when he was here yesterday afternoon."

"That's good, ma'am. We know about that. The photo you gave to Chief Morris has been shown to the people who formed the search parties this morning. We have also seen it but it is still in the possession of Chief Morris. Do you have another photo you can let us have?"

"Yes, of course."

While Patricia is out of the room to get a photo, Gerald returns, faster than they had hoped or expected, to the living room. He is carrying a large tray containing a teapot, three cups with saucers, creamer and sugar bowl along with some teaspoons, a dinner plate filled with buttered toast and three small side plates. He places the tray onto the coffee table and asks, "Where's Patricia?"

"She has gone to get us a recent photo of her daughter," Officer Owens responds.

"While you are here, I have a few questions for you, sir," Inspector Fletcher says. "Do you live here with your daughter and grand-daughter?"

"No, sir, I do not. I live out of town. I live north of here in Elliot Lake."

"I see. But do you visit here often?"

"Yes, I am retired and I try to get here as often as I can. My daughter is a doctor and she works long hours all week. She has a baby-sitter to care for Susan when she is not in school but she doesn't need the sitter when I'm here. It's not always as often as I would like but when I'm able to be here I look after the house. I also spend time with my grand-daughter and look after her. It's been hard for my daughter since her husband died. It's not easy for a woman raising a child on her own."

Just then Patricia returns to the living-room. She carries a photo album and holds it open as she offers it to Inspector Fletcher. "There are so many beautiful photos. I can't decide which one to give you. Please, just take whichever one you want."

Inspector Fletcher accepts the album then passes it to Officer Owens to make the photo selection.

"Mrs. Donnelly," he asks, "Susan is an only child?"

"Yes, she is all I have in this world. Please find her for me."

"I would like the name and address of your baby-sitter."

"Yes, her name is Nan Barton. She's a wonderful older woman and she's just like a grand-mother to my little girl. My own mother died when

I was just a child. And since my husband died his parents rarely visit us. "

"You are a physician?"

"I am."

"My apologies. We should have been addressing you as Dr. Donnelly; not Mrs. Donnelly. Doctor, do you have any idea what has occurred? Any thoughts as to where your daughter may be?"

"None. I put her to bed last night around nine p.m. School is out for the summer and it doesn't get dark until so late at night and this is why I let her stay up so late. And I value her company in the evenings. I never let her outside to play after seven p.m. unless I am outside in the backyard with her. I like her to have some quiet time before her bedtime. I find it helps her to get to sleep much easier."

"Do you have a boyfriend, Doctor? I'm sorry to pry into your personal life but this is something I have to ask."

"No, no boyfriend. I haven't wanted to date anyone since my husband died. No, it's just Susie and me."

"And your father?" Officer Owens interjected?

"He visits when he can. It's a long drive from Elliot Lake but he comes fairly often and when he does I cancel my baby-sitter. Dad looks after things here in the house and takes care of Susie until I get home from the office or the hospital.

At this point Inspector Fletcher stands up from the couch. Officer Owens follows suit. "We will have more but those are all my questions for now Doctor Donnelly. With your permission, Officer Owens will remain here with you. If your daughter has been kidnapped we expect there will be a ransom call. Officer Owens will set up the equipment in order to trace any calls that come through."

"I have everything I need in here," Officer Owens says as she taps the suitcase.

"I wondered what that suitcase was for," Gerald says.

"Yes," Inspector Fletcher responds, "Now that everything is under control I will be on my way but I will soon be in touch, Doctor. Oh, by the way, Mr. Gagnon, do you plan to stay in Fairmont for some time?"

"Yes, sir, I do. However if I am assured that Officer Owens will be here with my daughter I may make a quick trip home to Elliot Lake to pick up some of my clothing and other personal things that I will need while I am staying here. Is there any problem if I leave to make a trip home?"

"No, no problem. That will be fine, sir. And now I will be on my way. Thank you for the tea."

Gerald shows the Inspector to the door. When he returns to the living-room Officer Owens is not there. Patricia is alone in the room, again huddled in the armchair.

"Where has she gone?" he asks.

"She is setting up her equipment on the dining-room table."

"I see," he says. "Patricia, will you be okay if I leave now? I'll be back here with you again tomorrow. I just need to pick up a few things."

"Don't leave me alone, Dad."

"But you're not alone, Patricia. Officer Owens will be here and how would it be if I give Heather a call and ask her to come stay with you for a bit? Just until I return, will that be okay?" Without waiting for her response he picks up the phone, "Hello Heather. Yes, this is Gerald."

"I can't speak to you right now, Gerald. An RCMP Inspector is here to ask me some questions."

"Oh, I see. Heather, once your interview is over would you mind coming over here and spending some time with Patricia? I need to make a quick run home to Elliot Lake but I will return tomorrow. Can you do this for me please?"

"Yes, Gerald. It's not a good idea to leave Patricia alone. You stay there until I come over and I'll be there as soon as I can."

"Thank you, Heather."

Gerald returns the wireless phone to its cradle. "Heather is coming over soon. In the meantime you have Officer Owens here. If you are okay, Patricia, I will be on my way. The sooner I leave the sooner I can return."

Patricia says nothing. Her audible sigh says it all. She watches as her father leaves the house. Getting up from her chair she looks through the living-room window and observes the reporters swarming around her father's Jeep Grand Cherokee as he tries to back out of the driveway.

She does not notice Chief Morris, in his green Chevrolet Impala, following behind Gerald. An ordinary green Chevy will attract the attention of no one; certainly not that of all the TV reporters and certainly not that of Gerald Gagnon.

THIRTEEN

THIRTEEN:

The Investigation Continues

Inspector Fletcher leaves Patricia Donnelly's home by the front door. Surveying the madness of TV reporters, cameras, and crowds of people gathering out front on the sidewalk and boulevard he decides to take a different route. He slips around to the back of the Donnelly house, crosses their backyard until he comes to the high fence dividing the Donnelly yard from that of the Martins.

He works his way up the other side of the Donnelly house then hops the low fence that gives him access into the front yard. He then turns right onto the front lawn of Heather Martin and makes his way to her front door.

Heather is home alone when the doorbell rings. Peering through the living room window she can see a tall man in a grey suit standing near the front door. Though not in uniform there is something about him that makes her think he looks like a cop. Ernie and the boys are out with the search party. She wishes she wasn't home alone. He looks like a cop, she thinks, but what if he isn't? What if he is a reporter? Worse than that, what if he is the kidnapper? She doesn't know whether to answer the door or not.

The doorbell rings again.

Hoping she is making the right decision she opens the door and looks up into the face of a man she does not recognize. She doesn't recognize the badge he holds in his hand either but it looks official and it does look authentic. "Yes?" is all she says.

"Mrs. Martin?"

"I'm Doctor Martin."

"My apology Doctor Martin. I am RCMP Inspector Raymond Fletcher. I have just a few questions to ask of you. May I come in?"

Heather ushers the Inspector into her livingroom where he chooses the largest armchair in the room to sit. She watches him draw a notebook and pen out of his pocket and she watches him cross his legs and get comfortable in the chair before she sits down across from him on the chesterfield. She feels alone and vulnerable. She wishes Ernie was home with her.

"I have just a few questions to ask you. I won't keep you long, Doctor Martin. To begin, I understand you are a close friend of Patricia Donnelly?"

Before Heather can respond to his question the phone rings. She looks at Inspector Fletcher who nods assent. She picks up the wireless receiver from its pocket on the side table. He listens to her side of the conversation.

"I can't speak to you right now, Gerald. An RCMP Inspector is here to ask me some questions…………..Yes, Gerald. But it's not a good idea to leave Patricia alone. You stay there until I come over and I'll be there as soon as I can.

She replaces the receiver and stares into the questioning face of the Inspector.

"I could not help but overhear, Doctor. You were speaking with Gerald Gagnon?"

"Yes."

"May I ask what it was he wanted?"

"He wants me to come over to stay with Patricia. He is going back to Elliot Lake to pick up his things."

"Oh, yes," the inspector says. "That comes as no surprise to me. Now, Doctor, if I may, I understand you live here with your husband?"

"Yes, but he's not home. He's out with the search party and so are my boys."

"I see. Your boys? How many boys do you have?"

"I have three sons."

"Their names and ages?"

"My oldest is William at seventeen; Harold is fifteen and Gordon is thirteen."

"I see, and they are with your husband on the search party?"

"I didn't want them to go but, yes, that's where they are."

"And you had a reason for not wanting them to go, ma'am?"

"I was just trying to protect them but they are okay. As long as they stay with my husband I'm okay with them being on the search party."

"Your husband, what is his profession, doctor?"

"Ernie is a lawyer."

"Since your boys are much older than the missing child I don't expect they would have much contact with her?"

"No, that's where you're wrong. Susie was often coming over here wanting Gordie, my youngest, to play with her. It drove Gordie nuts. He didn't want her around. He just didn't want to be bothered with her and he would tell her to go home."

"And your other children?"

"No, they had no time for Susie but my oldest boy William did say he sometimes felt sorry for her being an only child with no father. It was Harold who said that she still had her grandfather though so he didn't feel so sorry for her."

"I see."

"I was surprised though when Gordon told me that Susan didn't like her grandfather. Gordie said Susie told him that her grandfather was weird."

"Did you find out why she said her grandfather was weird?"

"No, that's about it."

"You are a good friend of Doctor Donnelly?"

"Yes, we work together at the hospital. We're neighbours and, sure, we are friends."

At this point Inspector Fletcher stands up from the couch. "Thank you for your time, Doctor Martin. If I have any further questions I will be in touch with you."

Heather shows the Inspector to the door. Just before he leaves he asks, "You will be going next door now to Doctor Martin's house?"

"I will, yes."

"I see," is all the Inspector has to say about that.

Heather closes the door. She goes into her kitchen. After rummaging in a drawer she withdraws a small pad of paper and a pen. She writes a note, tears the small sheet from the pad and sticks it up on the fridge door with a magnet. *I'm over at Patricia's* is all the note says.

Heather is surprised when she knocks on Patricia's door to have it opened by a woman she has never seen before in her life. "Who are you?" she asks.

"I am Officer Owens of the RCMP. And who are you?"

"I'm Heather Martin. Patricia's father phoned me earlier and asked me to come stay with Patricia because he wants to return to Elliot Lake."

"Come in, Heather," Patricia shouts from the living-room. "It's okay, Officer Owens."

"Where is Gerald?" Heather asks upon her entry into the living-room.

"He wanted to go home to pick up some fresh clothes and stuff. He will be back here tomorrow."

Heather is annoyed. "I told him to stay with you until I got here. What was his big rush to go anyway?"

"I don't know why he was so anxious to leave, Heather. I didn't want him to go at all but I couldn't convince him to stay."

"Any news of Susie, Patricia?"

"Nothing Heather. Not even a call for ransom.

"Strange, very strange." Then, "Sorry Patricia, I didn't mean to start you crying again. I'm so very sorry."

Heather reaches out and embraces her friend who remains huddled in her chair.

FOURTEEN

FOURTEEN:

Just a Hunch

Inspector Fletcher leaves the home of Doctor Martin. Crossing the front lawns he makes his way toward Number Seven Crabapple Court, the home of the Kovacs family. He rings the doorbell and does not wait long for the door to be opened by a middle-aged man.

"What do you want?" the man asks rather gruffly.

Inspector Fletcher introduces himself then asks, "Are you Daniel Kovacs?"

"I am."

"I have a few questions to ask of you and your wife. May I come in?"

Again Inspector Fletcher is ushered into a living-room. He can't help but notice the beauty of this home. All the homes on Crabapple Court are luxurious but the centre hall plan of this gorgeous Georgian home he finds especially impressive.

In the large living-room Daniel Kovacs introduces the Inspector to his wife. "This is my wife, Marsha Kovacs, Inspector."

"How do you do," she replies indicating with her hand that he should be seated.

He chooses to sit in a comfortable upholstered chair and asks the two if they will please sit across from him on the sofa. "If you have no objection I will put my questions to both of you," he says.

"That's fine," Daniel replies.

"I have no objection," Marsha answers.

So begins Inspector Fletcher's questioning of the Kovacs.

***

Meanwhile Officer Madison Morris drives his green Chevrolet behind the dark black Jeep Grand Cherokee. The vehicle is about three years old, Madison thinks. And he isn't surprised to see that Gerald Gagnon is driving an SUV. Those northern winter roads are best traversed in an SUV, not that Elliot Lake is that far north but to Madison, who rarely leaves the little Town of Fairmont, it seems a long way from home.

Officer Madison Morris is a close-mouthed kind of character. He isn't the kind of guy who needs to think out loud. He trusts his hunches but even these he keeps to himself until they are proven to be either accurate or, if proven otherwise, they are tossed out like last night's stale beer.

Madison has a hunch about Gerald Gagnon; one he doesn't even mention to his partner, Nick. That morning while Nick is working with the volunteers and organizing the search party, Madison puts on his thinking cap. He can't help but notice that Gerald Gagnon does not show up to help with the search party. Although he says otherwise to his partner, that seems odd to him. If it was my granddaughter, he thinks, I'd be out there leading the pack.

And when he talks with Patricia and Gerald he notices that the grandfather is as cool as a cucumber. Again that doesn't sit right with Madison. If your grand-daughter goes missing you either shout or cry. You at least show some kind of raw emotion. No, Gerald is too cool, too calm and collected. That just does not seem natural to Madison.

He has been told that when Gerald is in Fairmont, he is Susie's primary caregiver while Patricia is at work. But Madison can't get little Gordon Martin's words out of his head. He remembers Gordie saying, "Susie isn't too crazy about her grandfather. She said the old guy is kind of weird."

Now why would a little girl say something like that about her grandfather, Madison wonders. He also remembers that when he had talked to the Cavendish family in Number Nine it was Susie's little playmate, eight-year-old Robert who had asked his mother, "Why did she run away?" He remembers that Marian Cavendish had told him that her boy had asked that question. Why would the kid think Susie had run away?

Madison also remembers that even Patricia Martin had told him that Susie doesn't like being left with her grandfather. What were her exact words? That's right, Susie had told her mother, "I don't want to be with Grandad."

Madison questions Patricia about that but she tells him that she never did know why Susie would say such a thing. They seem to get along well together, Patricia says.

All these thoughts bounce around in Madison's head as he follows Gerald Gagnon's car along the city streets. He's taking an odd route to go to Elliot Lake, he thinks.

Madison has stocked his old green Chevy well. He has gassed up and has a full tank. He is all set and prepared to follow Gerald up to either his house or his cabin in Elliot Lake.

But they are travelling in the wrong direction. Soon they are getting closer to Toronto. Where is this guy going, he wonders. But he does not have too much longer to be in suspense.

Gerald signals to make a left turn. He waits for the road to clear of traffic and then he drives into a driveway that leads him into the parking lot of a Holiday Inn. Madison is totally surprised but he follows right behind him.

He parks a short distance away from him. He watches as Gerald parks his SUV, then gets out of the car and walks to the entrance of the hotel.

What on earth is going on, Madison asks of himself. Does Mr. Gagnon have a girlfriend waiting for him in a hotel room?

He is going to follow him into the hotel but again he has a hunch and decides to follow it. He will stay with the car and see where this decision leads.

FIFTEEN

FIFTEEN:

Questioning of The Kovacs continues

RCMP Inspector Fletcher chooses to sit in a comfortable upholstered chair and asks the two if they will please sit across from him on the sofa. "If you have no objection I will put my questions to both of you," he says.

"That's fine," Daniel Kovacs replies.

"I have no objection," Marsha answers.

"Mr. Kovacs, may I start with this question? What is your profession?"

"Sure. I'm a dentist here in Fairmont. I have my office over on Main Street."

"And is Susan Donnelly one of your patients, Dr. Kovacs?"

"Nope, Fairmont is a small place but we do have another dentist in town. Neither Susan nor her mother are my patients."

"I see, but of course they are your neighbours. Do you have any other relationship with either of the Donnellys?

"No, none whatsoever. We say good morning or hello if we meet on the street, that's about it."

"Okay and what about Dr. Donnelly's father? Are you familiar with Gerald Gagnon?"

"Nope, never met the man."

"Okay, thank you, Doctor Kovacs."

Shifting just a little in his chair, Inspector Fletcher smiles and begins to direct his questions to Marsha Kovacs. Before beginning his questioning he cannot help but notice that she does not appear to be as calm and collected as her cooperative husband. He notices the tiny beads of perspiration on her forehead, the trembling of her bottom lip and he also notices that she does her best to escape eye contact whenever he speaks to her.

"Just a few questions for you now, Mrs. Kovacs, if you don't mind."

He accepts her silence as acquiescence.

"I understand you are a psychotherapist?"

"Yes, I am."

"And where is your professional office located?"

"Downstairs. My office is here at home in the basement."

"Oh, I see. Well, that must be very nice for you not having to travel to work."

"Yes."

"Mrs. Kovacs, who are your clients?"

"I'm not at liberty to divulge that information, I'm sorry."

"Let me put my question to you this way then. Perhaps it will make things easier for you. I have been informed that you draw your client base from three sources; the first being the Prison Board, the second being the Drug and Alcohol Rehabilitation Centre and the third being the Welfare Department. Am I correct in my understanding?"

"Yes."

"What I would like from you, Mrs. Kovacs, is a list of your clients' names and their contact information."

"No, I'm sorry. I have therapist/client confidentiality to take into consideration. I cannot give you that information."

"I understand. In that case I will need to return at a later time with a search warrant."

Inspector Fletcher cannot help but notice that the sweat beads on the forehead of Marsha Kovacs are turning into little rivulets which she swipes at with her hand. Her lips quiver when she speaks; both lips, not just the bottom one. Yes, he can see that her uneasiness is increasing the more she is questioned. Still he continues.

"Do you and your husband have any children, Mrs. Kovacs?"

"No."

"Do you like children?"

"Yes, of course I like children."

Dr. Kovacs interjected, "Inspector, what does my wife's liking of children have to do with the missing Donnelly girl?"

"Do you like children, Dr. Kovacs?"

"What?" he responds. "Yes, of course I do. We both like children. We just were not blessed with any of our own, that's all."

"Mrs. Kovacs, how do you feel about not having any child of your own?"

He accepts her blank stare as her answer.

"Mrs. Kovacs, have you ever considered the idea of borrowing someone else's child?"

At this point Daniel Kovacs stands up from the couch, shakes his fist in the air and shouts, "Inspector, you are way out of line here! What kind of crazy questions are these to ask of us? No, we do not consider borrowing the children of others. You are suggesting very shady things about my wife. If you knew her, you would not be making these ridiculous accusations. My wife is a good woman. Her practices are highly ethical and straightforward. She sings in the church choir every Sunday, for God's sakes."

"Please be seated, Mr. Kovacs. My apologies for upsetting you. These questions need to be asked. And just one more question if you don't mind. Did you ever consider adopting a child, Mr. Kovacs?"

"No, I did not," is his curt reply.

Inspector Fletcher shifts in his chair and feels just a little uncomfortable as he speaks again to Mrs. Kovacs. "I apologize, ma'am. I did not mean to make you cry."

Marsha Kovacs does not speak. Tears cover her face like a blanket. She knows what it is like to be barren; to yearn for a child. The more she thinks of her neighbour Patricia Donnelly and the great loss she is enduring, the more she sobs. She cannot imagine what it must be like to have a child only to lose it. She cannot imagine that heartbreaking yearning.

Inspector Fletcher has no inkling as to the cause or the source of Mrs. Kovacs' sobbing. He thinks it very strange. She offers him no explanation.

He stands and thanks them both for their co-operation and states that he will be returning soon with a warrant to examine her client records.

Daniel shows him to the door.

Left alone in the living-room, Marsha allows her tears to flow.

SIXTEEN

SIXTEEN:

Inspector Fletcher and the Cavendish Family

When he leaves Number Seven Crabapple Court, Inspector Raymond Fletcher does not feel well. It isn't his style to upset women and make them cry. He wonders if he is losing his touch. Maybe he has been at this job for too long. He does not feel like meeting another family but it is still relatively early in the day and the Cavendish home is right next door to the Kovacs. Better to get it all done, he decides.

Using his cell phone he calls in his request for search warrant for the examination of Marsha Kovacs' psychotherapy client files. Having done that, he crosses the lawns and makes his way toward Number Nine, the home of the Cavendish family.

As he approaches the house he thinks it is a bit odd looking. His observation suggests that perhaps it has once been an attractive ranch style bungalow but it seems to have many bits and pieces, large ones of course, tacked on here, there and everywhere. He notices the addition closest to the Kovacs' home. It is not attractive. Compared to the other impressive, luxurious homes on Crabapple Court, the home of the Cavendish family simply does not measure up. Sure, it is as large, perhaps even larger, the Inspector notices but it just doesn't have the same class as the other homes that share the same street.

Before he rings the doorbell the Inspector stands on the verandah, a beautiful verandah that circles the entire house, and as he stands there he stares out at the large number of people still milling about on the boardwalk as well as on the tree-blossomed boulevard. He sees the signature vans from all the local TV stations. He sees the cameras and the reporters with their microphones in hand. He thinks about the volunteers out with the search parties and hopes they are having more success than he is.

He turns toward the door and rings the doorbell.

A frumpish older woman answers the door. Inspector Fletcher assumes she is the Cavendish housekeeper. "May I see Mr. or Mrs. Cavendish, please?" he asks.

"I'm Mrs. Cavendish," she replies.

Raymond quickly swallows his surprise and introduces himself. "Mrs. Cavendish, I am RCMP Inspector Raymond Fletcher. May I please come in to ask you a few questions?"

"Is this about the missing girl?"

"Yes, ma'am."

"Can't tell you nuthin' but you can come in if you want, sure. Come on in."

"Thank you, ma'am."

Marian leads the Inspector into their large but cluttered living-room. "Sit yourself down anywhere," she says before yelling, "George, we got company!"

Inspector Fletcher moves a few newspapers aside and sits down on a swivel rocker. Within a few minutes he is surprised to see coming into the living-room a very short, very fat man with a lit cigar dangling from his lips.

The Inspector has been informed that the Cavendish family is the wealthiest family, not only in Fairmont, but also for miles around. He had expected to be met by a man more closely resembling the class and stature of the residents of Crabapple Court with whom he is already acquainted. He isn't prepared for this vertically challenged, down-to-earth, balding fellow wearing blue jeans and a red plaid shirt.

George Cavendish extends his hand. Inspector Fletcher stands up from the swivel chair and shakes the man's hand. He cannot help but notice that the man has a powerful grip.

"What can I do ya for?" George asks, while making himself comfortable on the cluttered sofa.

The Inspector sits down once again on the swivel chair and swiveling it around to face the home owner, he answers, "I'm here to ask you a few questions about the missing Donnelly girl. I'm sure by now you have heard something about this?"

"Yes, sir, I have. We got all the newspapers," he says indicating his paper-strewn couch. "And all them people milling about on the boulevard and the boardwalk are something a man can't ignore no matter how hard he tries."

"Yes, I'm sure that is a fact."

"A fact that can't be denied. Now it's a sad thing that kid has gone missing but I have to tell you I don't know a thing about it except what I've read in the papers and the little I've heard on the TV."

By this time Mrs. Cavendish has left the room and just the two men remain in the living-room.

"You have a family, Mr. Cavendish?"

"You're darn right I do. I've got me three kids and they're good kids too except for the oldest one. Thomas is an irresponsible, stupid boy that I'm half ashamed to call my own but, as bad as he is, he wouldn't hurt no little kid. No, none of my family knows anything about this disappearance."

"I'd like to speak to all your family members if you don't have any objection, Mr. Cavendish."

"Nope, I've got no problem with that. Marian!" he bellows. "Come on in here to the living-room and bring all the kids with you!"

The Inspector doesn't have to wait long before the frumpy Mrs. Cavendish returns to the room. Trailing behind her are the three children. All good looking kids, Raymond notes and from what he can see they are well-behaved too. They enter the room and settle themselves in the two sofas that are set kitty-corner opposite the swivel chair in which he sits.

It is Mrs. Cavendish who introduces the children to him. "Starting with the oldest, this is my son Thomas. He's nineteen. Next is my daughter Dolores who is sixteen. The youngest boy is Robert who just turned eight years old last month."

"Hello children, my name is Inspector Fletcher. Do you mind if I ask you a few questions about Susan Donnelly? I take it you all know who she is?"

"I know her," young Robert speaks up. "Susie ran away, didn't she?"

"I don't know, Robert. But tell me, what makes you think she might have run away?"

"No reason. She's gone aint she? So she must have run away."

"Oh, I see. Do you think Susie was happy in her home, Robert? Kids don't usually run away if they are happy, right?"

"Susie was happy enough with her Mom but she didn't have no Dad. All she had was her grandad and she didn't like him."

"How do you know she didn't like him, Robert?"

"She told me; that's how I know."

"And did she tell you why she didn't like her grandfather?"

"Nope."

"I see. Well, thank you, Robert. Is there anything else that any of you children can tell me about why you think Susan Donnelly might be missing or about where you think she might be?"

Sixteen-year-old Dolores is the only one to speak up. "She's a lot younger than me; a lot younger than all of us really. Robert is the only one close to her age. He's the only one who played with her."

"I see, thank you, Dolores."

Inspector Fletcher turned his attention to the eldest child, Thomas. Tom Cavendish was very nervous. He wasn't about to let anybody know the truth of what had happened. He hadn't been home long and he needed to figure out a way to get back to his car. He would need to walk back and somehow disguise the fact that he is carrying a shovel. Then out of the blue it dawned on him. He'd carry the shovel in his guitar case. Tom was unaware that his self-proclaimed cleverness had brought a smile to his lips.

"You find this amusing, Tom?"

He was snapped out of his reverie by Inspector Fletcher's question.

"What?"

"I said do you find this amusing, Tom?"

"No, sir."

"Thomas, I've been informed that you sometimes like to spend some time around the school yard. I hear you sometimes hang out around the play area at the elementary school. Is there any truth in what I've been told?"

"That's a load of rubbish! Who told you that? Whoever it is, they're lying through their teeth. And if I find out who it is I'll bust his friggin' teeth!"

"Thomas!" George Cavendish roars. "You watch your tongue!" Then to the Inspector he says, "I told you this one was no good. Don't know what we are going to do with him but I can vouch for the fact that he has nothing to do with the little girl you're here asking about."

"You're damn right!" Thomas asserts. "Damn cops blame me for every damn thing that goes wrong in this stinkin' town! I don't know nuthin about this kid and that's the God honest truth!"

"Mrs. Cavendish," the Inspector continues, "Is there anything further you can tell me about the disappearance of this little girl?"

"I wish there was, Inspector. I don't even know the little kid really or her mother. But I heard through the grapevine that the poor woman's been through more than enough what with losing her mother when she was just a kid herself and then her husband dying at such a young age. It must be tough for her being a single mom and now to have her kid disappear like that, I can't imagine what the poor woman is going through. Maybe I should go over and visit with her. What do you think of that idea, Inspector? Do you think it would help if I dropped in on her, maybe take over a plate of food?"

Before the Inspector has a chance to answer the question, Mr. Cavendish shouts, "No! Marian, I say no! You don't take no plate of food nowhere! I got me enough problems with the people in this town. I slave trying to collect my rents on all my properties and not only that but I have to deal with all those mill workers. I got me enough problems and I don't want you to go looking for more."

"George, I was just thinking of being a little neighbourly."

"We don't need no neighbourly nuthin',", George sputters. "Neighbours mind their own business and we mind ours. That's the way it's always been and I don't see no reason for any change."

"But George –

"Enough Marian. I said that's enough!" Then turning to Inspector Fletcher, George asks, "You got any more questions for my kids?"

"Not at this time, no, sir."

"Then go on, you kids, all of you! Skidaddle! Get out of here and leave us adults to talk."

The children all leave the room. They are quiet all but Thomas who cannot resist responding to his father, "Gladly!"

"Smart ass kid!" George states. "Inspector, do you have any more questions of my wife?"

At that point Inspector Fletcher stands up from the swivel chair. "No, sir," he says. "In fact, I think that's all I have for anyone here at this time. If I should have any further questions for any of your family I will be in touch with you, sir. Thank you for your cooperation and, Mrs. Cavendish, thank you too."

"You're welcome," she says.

"I'll see you out," George offers. He walks to the door with the Inspector. Together they stand on the verandah for a few minutes surveying the crowd that seems larger than ever by now. "Can't see why they are all just hanging around here like this. Don't they have any honest work to do?" George complains. "Lighting candles and singing all those stupid songs, why don't they all just go home and mind their own business?"

"Some people are naturally drawn to tragedy, sir," the Inspector replies. "It's a sad state of affairs. Everyone is concerned about the disappearance of the little girl."

"Yep, there's something shady behind all this. That's a fact. I hope you catch the bugger that kidnapped the kid. Good day to you, sir." George turns back into his house and closes the door.

Inspector Fletcher remains on the porch for a little while longer. He thinks of all the families he has questioned. Only one family to go, he realizes, and I'm no further ahead. I've got no solid suspects; no glimmer of any motive. He looks at his watch and decides there is still time to visit the last house on the street. He withdraws his notebook from his pocket once again and reads, Number Eleven Crabapple Court, The Colletti Family.

He steps down off the verandah and once again makes his way across the front lawns until he steps into the front yard of a beautiful big house with a massive front entrance. He looks up and appreciates the multi-paned windows that run along the second storey. He is impressed with the huge white pillars that support the roof over the home's front entrance. The pillars remind him a little of the southern mansions he has seen in movies over the years. He has to pinch himself to be reminded that he is still in the little town of Fairmont, Ontario.

Once more he rings the doorbell. This time the door is opened by a young black woman wearing a maid's uniform. George bets this is the one and only maid that lives and works in Fairmont but all he says is, "Good afternoon, is Mr. or Mrs. Colletti at home?"

"Yes, sir. And who should I say is calling?"

Raymond withdraws a business card from his pocket, hands it to her and says, "Please tell them I am RCMP Inspector Raymond Fletcher and I would like a few moments of their time."

"Yes, sir," she says and shuts the door in his face. Raymond stands on the step and waits. He doesn't need to wait long."

The maid returns and invites him in. "Mr. and Mrs. Colletti will receive you in the living-room. Just follow me, sir."

"Thank you," he says and follows her through a massive and elegantly decorated foyer into a beautiful living-room filled with antique-looking furniture. The walls are decorated with lavish, large gilt framed paintings. Raymond is no art connoisseur but he wouldn't be a bit surprised to learn that the paintings are originals.

When he enters the room he is greeted by a woman that he guesses to be in her late fifties or early sixties. She is impeccably dressed in a stylish, tailored summer slacks suit in a soft shade of green; one for which he knows his wife would willingly give her right arm. "Inspector Fletcher," she says, "please do come in."

"Thank you." The Inspector shakes her proffered hand and turns to shake hands with the gentleman in the room.

"Welcome Inspector, I'm Mario Colletti and you have met my wife, Annette. What can we do for you, sir?"

"I have just a few questions for you and your wife, sir. As you may have guessed we are investigating the disappearance of your neighbour's little girl."

"A tragedy," Mrs. Colletti murmurs. "That poor child and that poor mother! I have two daughters of my own and five beautiful grandchildren. I can't for a moment imagine the hell that woman is enduring. Ever since I heard about the child's disappearance I have been praying for the family. Please, won't you sit down, Inspector? And can I offer you a cold drink?"

"No, thank you. And I won't keep you or your husband too long today. I have just a few questions." He sits down on one of the chairs across from the couple who sit side by side on what looks like a loveseat.

"I'll start with you, Mr. Colletti. How well do you know the Donnelly family?"

"Don't know them at all. They live a couple houses away from us. They're at Number Five if I'm not mistaken. I hear she's a doctor but she's neither my doctor nor my wife's. We don't socialize with our neighbours. Don't get me wrong, we're not rude or anything. I say good morning or good day whatever the case may be if I see any of my neighbours but that's where I draw the line. I've got no time for socializing with neighbours. My work keeps me busy."

"I see, and what about you, Mrs. Colletti? Do you know the family?"

"No, not really, Inspector. My own children are all grown up and living in Toronto. That's where my grandchildren are too so it's not like my grandchildren had a chance to get to know the little girl. Sure, sometimes I would see her as she was on her way to school or maybe out playing with that little Cavendish boy, Robert. They live right next door and so, of course, sometimes I would see little Suzie if she came over to play with Robert."

"Well, thank you, Mrs. Colletti and you too, sir. I'm sorry to have taken up your time. But, oh, yes, I understand you have a maid or a housekeeper. That would be the lady who answered the door?"

"Yes," Mrs. Colletti says, "that would be Annie. Annie Benjamin is our housekeeper."

"I would like a word with Annie if you don't mind, Mrs. Colletti."

"Oh, of course, Inspector. I'll get her."

At that point Mr. Colletti stands up and once again shakes hands with the Inspector. "Sir, if you have no further use for me I'll get back to work. Time is money, you know."

"Yes, of course. Thank you for your time, Mr. Colletti."

SEVENTEEN

SEVENTEEN:

Meet Annie Benjamin

For a few minutes Raymond sits alone in the impressive luxury of the Colletti's living-room. Of all the homes he has visited today he decides this one is his favourite. He is admiring the elaborate paintings hanging on the wall but stands when Mrs. Colletti returns with her housekeeper.

"Inspector," she says, "this is Annie Benjamin, our housekeeper."

"Hello Ms. Benjamin. I hope you won't mind answering a few questions for me."

"No, sir, but I don't know nuthin', sir. Honest I don't."

"Ms. Benjamin, do you have children of your own?"

"I do. I have my little Arabella is all."

"And how old is Arabella?

"She is seven; eight next month."

"Arabella then is almost the same age as the missing child, Susan. Did your little girl ever play with Susan?"

"Oh, no, sir. I never bring my child to work with me. Never. Mrs. Colletti can vouch for that."

"I see. And, Mrs. Benjamin, who takes care of your daughter while you are here working for the Colletti family?"

The Inspector notices the somber dark cloud that hovers about Annie's worried eyes when he asks that question. She lowers her face and stares at her hands which begin to fidget in her lap. "That would be Ronald," she almost whispers.

"Did you say Robert?"

"No, sir, I said that would be Ronald."

"I see. And who is Ronald, Ms. Benjamin? Is Ronald your husband?"

"No, we aren't married. Ronald, he is just my boyfriend."

"And what can you tell me about Ronald? Does he come here to the home of the Colletti's at all?"

"Well, sometimes he drives over this way and picks me up after work to drive me home. But not very often; only sometimes."

"I see. And what is your address, Ms. Benjamin? I believe I would like to ask a few questions of your boyfriend. I take it he lives with you?"

"Yes, sir. You think Ronald did something to that little girl?" she asks.

"I don't know the answer to that question, Ms. Benjamin."

"Oh, Lord, do you think he would do something like that to my little girl?"

Inspector Fletcher is taken aback by what the housekeeper is asking. He doesn't really know what to make of it at all. He has to ask. "Ms. Benjamin, has your boyfriend done something he shouldn't do with your little girl?"

"No, sir and he better not; he just better not or so help me God I will kill him! They told me he hurt that other little girl a long time ago but I never knew if that was true or just a made-up lie."

Mrs. Colletti speaks up then. "Annie, maybe you better tell the Inspector everything you know."

By now Annie is in tears. "I don't really know nuthin' else about it, Annette. You know I've talked about this with you before and I've told you all I know."

"I know, Annie, but maybe you need to tell everything you know to this Inspector."

"You think my Ronald hurt that little Susie girl? Oh, my God, you think my Ronald is hurting my little Arabella?"

Inspector Fletcher realizes he is getting a lot more than he bargained for in this visit. At last, a real suspect, he thinks. He sits with Annie Benjamin and gathers all the information she is able to give to him about her boyfriend who is potentially a pedophile.

"Ms. Benjamin, what is Ronald's last name?"

"His last name is Thompson, Ronald Thompson."

He will leave this house and pay a visit to this Ronald Thompson but first he will run his name through the system to confirm that he is, in fact, a known sexual offender; a pedophile.

The crowds are still milling around beneath the Crabapple blossoms when Inspector Fletcher leaves the Colletti home. He walks down to the boardwalk and spends some time chatting with the OPP officers who are there helping out with crowd control. The search parties have returned. The child's whereabouts remain unknown.

Upon receiving this news he walks back up to Number Five. He has received no call from Officer Owens so it is safe to assume there has been no ransom call. He rings the bell and is surprised that when the door opens he is greeted by Dr. Heather Martin. "Come in, Inspector."

"Thank you."

"Inspector, the search party has returned and my family is at home now. If you are going to be here with Patricia I'd like to take this opportunity to get home and see how my boys are doing."

"Yes, no problem, Dr. Martin. Is Mrs. Donnelly asleep?"

"No, she's still sitting by the phone in the living-room. Officer Owens is there with her now."

"Again thank you. Yes, you go home to be with your family."

He enters the living-room and is surprised to see Mrs. Donnelly sitting beside Officer Owens on the sofa. They are looking through a photo album. "She was just two when this was taken. She was crazy about her Daddy and he loved her so much."

"I can see he was a very handsome man," Officer Owens says. She looks up when the Inspector enters the room. She gives her head a negative shake letting him know there has been no call for ransom.

"Good evening," he says. "Officer Owens, are you prepared to stay here until Dr. Martin returns? She has just gone to check on her family."

"You don't need to stay with me," Dr. Donnelly says.

"Oh, but we need someone to stay here in order to monitor in case a call should come through. Officer Owens, your replacement should be here within the hour. Are you okay to stay here until then?

"No, problem, boss."

"Then I will be on my way. Good evening ladies."

He leaves the Donnelly home and walks down the driveway to the sidewalk. It is just a short walk until he reaches his parked car. He feels good. At last he has a suspect. He has a very strong feeling that Ronald Thompson is his man. He will need to wait to get the results once the file is run through the system but it shouldn't be too long a wait. He can be patient. It has been a long day and he is tired. He will head home now to his modest suburban bungalow where he will share a simple meal with his wife.

He has visited each of the five luxurious homes on Crabapple Court but he decides he won't mention these visits to his wife. No point in making her feel jealous. No, he looks forward to a nice, quiet evening with his wife but first he needs to pass all his gathered information along to the rest of the team in his department.

EIGHTEEN

EIGHTEEN:

An Arrest is Made

Inspector Fletcher has been relaxing at home for less than three hours when he gets the call. He is in the middle of eating his supper; the delicious spaghetti bolognese his wife has prepared for him.

"Oh, no, not so soon!" she complains aloud when he hangs up the phone and explains he has to go out again.

"Sorry love, but I think we've got our man. At least we have enough information to bring him in for questioning."

"Well, you can at least finish your supper before you go."

But the Inspector is not listening to his wife. He is talking on the phone again, this time to his partner, Officer Owens.

"No," she says, "I talked to my replacement just a half hour ago and there has been no ransom call. Dr. Martin is spending the night with Dr. Donnelly. Everything is under control. The search parties will be organized again tomorrow, this time by the OPP first thing in the morning. There is still no hint as to the whereabouts of the child."

"I've learned that Ronald Thompson is a registered sex offender. He was arrested and charged six years ago. He did his time and has been on probation for the last year or so."

"And he's living with a woman who has a young daughter?"

"You got it!"

"Oh, my god!"

"Okay, so I'm going in to the office now. We will have him picked up and brought in for questioning very soon. I'll keep you posted."

***

Ronald is there in the kitchen when Annie returns. "I'm hot and I'm thirsty! Gimme another beer outa that fridge, Annie."

"Get it yourself, Ronald. Stop pestering me."

Moving quickly across the kitchen floor, Ronald raises his fist and cuffs it up just under her chin. "Woman, why you gotta back-talk me this way?"

Backed up against the kitchen wall Annie prepares herself for his punch. Bang! Bang! Bang! Bang! The loud thumping at the door saves her. Startled, Ronald lowers his fist and moves away from Annie and toward the back door of the house.

Bang! Bang! Bang! Louder this time.

"You expecting someone?" he asks.

Annie shakes her head. "No. Hurry up and answer that door, Ronald, before that noise is gonna wake up my baby."

He opens the door to two uniformed RCMP officers. "Ronald Thompson? Are you Ronald Thompson?" one asks.

"Why you want to know my name? I aint done nuthin'. Why you here to torment me like this?"

"You are wanted for questioning regarding the disappearance of Susan Donnelly."

"I don't know nuthin' about that little kid. I never even met the kid, I swear."

"It's just some routine questioning, sir," the second officer states. "Come with us now and there will be no need to cuff you."

Annie is grateful for the arrival of the police that evening. Because of them she will be on the receiving end of one less beating. After they take Ronald away she goes into her little girl's room. For a long time she sits quietly on the yellow painted chair beside her child's bed. She looks down upon her little girl's face, so soft and pretty; so trusting and vulnerable. She has to get away from him. She begins to plan. She needs a good plan.

NINETEEN

NINETEEN:

Aint Done Nuthin'

Inspector Fletcher is in his office. He is sitting behind his cluttered desk when the two officers bring Ronald Thompson in to him for questioning. The Inspector asks them to remain in the room throughout the examination.

"Sit there," the Inspector orders.

Ronald sits and stares at his interrogator. "I aint done nuthin'. Why you brought me in here like this?"

"I have just a few questions, sir, if you don't mind. May I have your full name please?

"Ronald Thompson."

"Do you have a middle name or initial, Mr. Thompson?"

"Nope, it's just Ronald Thompson."

"Okay. Now what can you tell me about the disappearance of Susan Donnelly?"

"I can't tell you nuthin'. I don't know nuthin'."

"Mr. Thompson, I understand you are a registered sex offender in the Province of Ontario."

"I was just taking a pee. I swear I was just taking a pee."

"You were arrested and you have served time."

"You gotta believe me. It was late at night. I was on my way home and I had to pee. There was nobody in the damn park that I could see. I peed up against the wall of a change room. I was on my way home but the cops arrested me. That's all there was to it. Now they call me a registered sex offender and all I did was take a pee."

And so the questioning continues. But in the end Inspector Fletcher does not have the evidence to make an arrest.

While all this is taking place Officer Madison Morris is still sitting in his Chevy parked in the Holiday Inn's guest parking lot. He is keeping his eye on the black Jeep Grand Cherokee but he is beginning to feel tired and discouraged. Gerald Gagnon is still in the Holiday Inn, probably with a woman, and Chief Morris guesses he isn't going to get sight of him before morning.

He is very tired. He decides to make a call to his partner, Officer Nick Taylor, to see what is happening back in Fairmont.

"Hi Nick, how goes it?"

"Still no sign of the kid, Maddy. The search has been called off now until morning. I heard the RCMP have picked up a guy for questioning but no arrest has been made. Where the heck are you anyway, Maddy?"

"I'm in the parking lot of the Holiday Inn on Nellis Street."

"What are you doing there?"

"I followed the kid's grandfather here. He's in the hotel now; kind of fishy I think since he told everyone he was going home to Elliot Lake.

"That does sound –

"Oh, oh, Nick! He's coming out of the hotel now. Oh, my God Nick! He's coming toward his car and he's got a kid with him!"

"What?"

"I'm going to follow. Nick, call Inspector Fletcher and tell him what's happening. I'll stay in touch with you. Get in your car Nick. I want to know you are not far behind me."

He watches as Gerald opens the passenger side door for the little girl. She seems to get into the car willingly enough. Gagnon walks around the front of the car to the driver's side, opens the door and within seconds he starts the car. When he pulls forward out of his parking spot Madison starts his engine. He will follow, not too closely, but close enough. He has no intention of letting this guy out of his sight.

Gagnon's SUV makes its way out of the city and onto Highway 400. He is heading north and Chief Morris figures that now he is on his way to Elliot Lake with his grand-daughter in tow. He calls Nick again. "Heading north on the 400 Nick. Are you far behind me?"

"Don't worry, I'll catch up Maddy. I'll use the siren if I have to."

"Don't use the siren near the grandfather, Nick. We don't want to make the arrest on the highway. We'll catch him when he gets to his house in Elliot Lake. Have you given all the info to the RCMP?"

"Yes, sir. I'm told that Inspector Fletcher is on his way."

"You gave him the Elliot Lake address of Gagnon's house?"

"Yep, I sure did."

"Okay, see you there."

TWENTY

TWENTY:

False Arrest

Five hours later Gerald Gagnon pulls into a driveway in Elliot Lake. Chief Morris parks just a short distance away further down the street. From his vantage point he watches as the old man walks around the car and opens the door for the little girl. He continues to watch as the grandfather holds the child's hand and walks to the front door of the house where he raises his free hand and knocks.

Believing that Gerald lives alone Chief Morris is surprised to see the door opened by a woman. He can't hear the words they exchange but watches while the two disappear inside the home.

Once they are out of his view Chief Morris gets out of his car. He doesn't have to wait long before Officer Taylor pulls up in the police car. And not far behind Taylor is an unmarked car driven by Inspector Fletcher. Travelling with Inspector Fletcher are two other members of his RCMP team.

The five officers work together. They circle and surround the building but it is Inspector Fletcher who knocks on the front door of the house. Gagnon opens the door and is shocked to see the Inspector.

"Inspector Fletcher, what are you doing here in Elliot Lake?" he asks.

Just then a woman's voice is heard calling, "Who is it Gerald?"

Fletcher is confused. "Who is the woman, Gerald? I understood you live here alone."

"Live here? I don't live here at all."

A pretty young woman in her thirties joins Gerald at the front door. "Yes, can I help you?" she asks.

"May I come in, ma'am?"

She looks at Gerald who nods his approval.

"Yes, come in. What is all this about?"

Fletcher enters the house followed closely behind by another RCMP Constable. Officers Morris and Taylor enter the house too.

"Where's the child?" Chief Morris demands.

"In the bedroom," the young woman answers. "What is your interest in my child?"

Chief Morris makes his way into the bedroom. The little girl is playing with some Barbie dolls.

"Hello Susie, may I sit with you for a little while?"

"Sure. You want to play? But my name is not Susie. My name is Carolyn," the little girl replies.

Chief Morris is surprised to say the least to learn that this is not the missing child. What kind of a blunder have we made, he wonders. He leaves the little girl in her room and returns to the living-room where Inspector Fletcher is carrying out his duties.

"Gerald Gagnon, you are under arrest for the kidnapping of seven-year-old Susan Donnelly."

"Are you crazy man? I don't know where my grand-daughter is!"

"Save it for the Judge!" Fletcher orders. Then to the RCMP Constables, "Cuff the prisoner."

Officer Taylor is a Cheshire cat.

Inspector Fletcher is happy. "Well done!" he says.

"Thank you, sir," the men reply.

Chief Morris can remain silent no longer. "Inspector!"

"Yes, Chief Morris. My thanks to you too. How is little Susie?"

"Sir, Susie is not here. The little girl says her name is Carolyn."

"Oh, my God! You think Gerald kidnapped Susie?" the pretty young woman asks. "You've made a big mistake here! Carolyn is my little girl. She has been staying at the Holiday Inn in Toronto with her Daddy, my husband Earl, who is there conducting some business. Earl called me yesterday and told me he was being detained there for another week. Gerald is our friend and also our next door neighbour. I knew he was out of town staying in Fairmont. He asked me to keep an eye on his house. I agreed and I asked him if he would pick Carolyn up at the Holiday Inn on his way home.

He was kind enough to do this favour for us. Otherwise I would have had to drive down to Toronto myself. Gerald agreed to stop in at the Holiday Inn to pick her up. He agreed to bring Carolyn home since he was coming this way anyway.

You've made a huge mistake. Gerald has done nothing wrong. I was expecting them. Earl phoned me from the Holiday Inn and told me that Gerald was on his way with Carolyn. I knew that Gerald was going to bring her home and then go to his own house to pick up his clothes before returning to his daughter's home in Fairmont.

Inspector Fletcher is shocked. "What? Gagnon, why didn't you say something?"

"You didn't give me a chance to say anything! Now will you take these cuffs off me?"

The Inspector gives the order. "Release him!"

The police cars parked on the street draw the attention of Gagnon's neighbours who start coming out onto their front lawns to see what is going on. Several of them watch as Gerald Gagnon leaves the home of his neighbour. They had all heard about the disappearance of Susan Donnelly.

"What's going on? Is the grandfather the culprit?" one asks.

"Sure looks that way. Why else would the cops be here?"

"Yep! Pervert!"

"Imagine that! The child's own grandfather! If that don't beat all!" another yells.

By now all the neighbours are assembled on one lawn right across the street from the parked police vehicles. "String 'em up!" one shrieks.

"He was a quiet neighbour, never caused no trouble," another says softly.

"It's the quiet ones you have to watch."

They observe as the police cars pull away. Gerald gets into his own car and pulls into his own driveway next door.

"Oh, so it isn't him after all!" one neighbour states.

"Didn't think it was him anyway," another says.

The neighbours take their time returning to their houses. "Well, you never know who does what in this world!"

"Never seen so much excitement in Elliot Lake since the mall collapse," they all agree.

TWENTY-ONE

TWENTY-ONE:

One Less Suspect

"Well, you sure led us on a wild good chase Morris!"

"Yes, sir, Inspector. I was so sure. When I saw Gagnon leaving the hotel with the little girl I just assumed it was the Donnelly kid. I guess I jumped the gun."

"I might have done the same thing myself, Chief Morris. Look at it this way; now we have one less suspect to deal with."

It is the second day of Susan Donnelly's disappearance. Search teams continue their vigilant effort but so far to no avail. Back in Fairmont the house at number five Crabapple Court is transformed into a mini police station. Two officers are there waiting to record the expected call from the unknown kidnapper. Patricia Donnelly is being kept under light sedation by Dr. Heather Martin who stayed overnight with her neighbour and friend.

Inspector Fletcher and the constables return to Fairmont as have the local police officers, Morris and Taylor. Gerald Gagnon is on his way after spending the night at his home in Elliot Lake.

"I'll stay with you, Patricia, until your dad gets here.

"Thank you, Heather. He left early this morning so he should be here around lunch time. I appreciate all you are doing for me."

Gerald arrives shortly before two p.m.

"Sorry for all they put you through, Dad. I have no idea why they suspected you of anything wrong."

"Nor I, Patricia, but I guess when they saw me leaving the hotel with little Carolyn in tow it is easy to understand they thought I was up to no good. I guess I would have been wise to mention to the police about the plan with the neighbour to bring the little girl back to Elliot Lake but I never dreamed I was a suspect in the first place. I had no idea they would be following me when I left the house here yesterday."

Just then the phone rings and everyone is silent. Officer Owens nods at Patricia to pick up the call.

"Hello," she says.

"Mrs. Donnelly?"

"Yes?"

"This is Annette Colletti, your neighbour."

"Yes, hello Annette."

"Patricia, my husband will shoot me for getting involved but there's something I feel I need to tell you."

"Yes, what is it, Annette?"

"My housekeeper Annie phoned me just a few minutes ago. She told me that her boyfriend, Ronald, has left town."

"Her boyfriend?"

"Yes, Patricia. The thing is her boyfriend is a registered pedophile. With your little girl's disappearance Annie became frantic thinking maybe Ronald has something to do with it. And she is so afraid that Ronald might be hurting her own little girl so she confronted him."

"Yes, does she think he has my Susie?"

"I don't know Patricia but that's why I am calling you. The police have already questioned him and they made no arrest. He returned home before Annie had a chance to leave so she ordered him to get out. She told me that when she confronted him Ronald threw some things around and then he left the house telling Annie he wouldn't be back."

"Oh, my! Thanks for telling me, Annette."

"I had to Patricia. I'm so very sorry for what you are going through. My husband will kill me for getting involved but I just couldn't keep this information to myself. I don't know if Ronald is the kidnapper but he sure needs to be checked out. He has left Annie but whether he has left town or not I have no idea. Annie hopes he has and she hopes he will never return but Patricia if he has your Susie – well, I hope and pray he does not but I had to tell you about this."

"Thanks again. I have to go now. I have to keep the line open in case he – well, in case someone calls." She hung up the phone.

"We've got it Doctor Donnelly!" Officer Owens offered thumbs up.

TWENTY-TWO

TWENTY-TWO:

Suspect – Ronald Thompson

Officer Owens filled Inspector Fletcher in on everything that Annette Colletti had said about Annie Benjamin's boyfriend, Ronald Thompson.

"We already questioned him and didn't have enough evidence to keep him," Owens says,

"Let's go pick him up again. Further questioning is definitely in order," Inspector Fletcher responds.

"From what we just heard from Mrs. Colletti he has already flown the coop."

"Officer Owens, get an all points bulletin out now for the capture of Ronald Thompson."

"Yes, sir," she says. Consider it done."

"I'm on my way now to the home of Annie Benjamin. Maybe hopefully she has some idea where Thompson is headed. You stay here Officer Owens in case we are barking up another wrong tree and you get a call for ransom."

"Yes, sir."

To Patricia Donnelly he says, "I'll be back later. In the meantime perhaps you can gather some photos of your daughter together. I think it's past high time we put a poster together and get it circulated."

"I'll help my daughter with that, Inspector."

"Good. Then I'm on my way but like I said, I'll be back later."

*

Inspector Fletcher and his team go in search of Ronald Thompson unaware that Tom Cavendish has done the evil deed. Hidden by the trees in the woods just outside of town the innocent child lay motionless in the trunk of a car.

Tom Cavendish knew he was a dumb ass. He should have had some Pez in his pocket as he had in the preceding days. It was an old trick he often used to get kids hooked on drugs. He would slip them a Pez initially and then later he would sell them something with a bigger kick. But he never sold to kids as young as Susie. Tom Cavendish knew he had acted like a fool giving the kid the drug but she was making so much noise he didn't know what else to do.

The way things were going in the school yard Tom knew that if he didn't find a way to shut this kid up he was going to be in big trouble. What brings the kid out so early in the mornings is a mystery to him. School is out for the summer. She has no business being here but here she is again demanding candy.

"I can't give you any candy today, Susan. The ones I have are just for big kids."

"I'm big enough!"

"You're not. Now scram! Beat it kid!"

"No. I say no and I mean no Tommy Cavendish!"

"What a stubborn little bugger you are kid!"

"Am not!"

He withdraws some packets from his pocket. They contain prescription pills of different shapes, sizes and colours. Choosing one pill from among the smallest he gives it to Susan who emulates the older children she has watched. She pops the pill into her mouth.

"Okay, kid, you got what you wanted now beat it!"

Susan turns away from the school yard and begins her trek home. She always manages to get back into her bedroom before her Mom knocks on her door in the morning. Tom's eyes follow her. He is shocked and surprised when he sees her fall to the ground.

Oh, my god! He runs toward her. Kneeling on the ground beside her he knows he has killed her. Oh, my god!

He looks in all directions. There is no one to be seen. Picking Susan up he carries her back through the school yard to his car that is parked just outside the school's gate. He lifts the hood of the trunk and gently rolls the child out of his arms and onto the trunk's floor. He shuts the hood, moves up to the driver's seat and heads for the woods just outside of town where he will bury her. He has no other choice.

The body of Susan Donnelly is trapped in the trunk. Tom tries to think straight as he drives out of town toward the woods.   When he feels he has driven far enough to avoid any search parties that might come looking for the kid he drives the car off the main road and onto a dirt road. He keeps driving until he feels he is far enough from the main road to avoid detection. He stops the car. Getting out of his vehicle he is satisfied that it is well hidden by the trees.

Then it suddenly dawns on him that he has no tools. Slapping his forehead he realizes his own stupidity. How can he bury the kid when he has no shovel to dig a hole? He knows he will have to return home to get what he needs.

Not wanting to drive the girl's body back into town in case he gets stopped for any reason he decides he will leave the car where it is and walk. He's afraid. He didn't mean to kill the kid. And now he's afraid he will get caught.

Leaving the car behind he begins walking. He arrives home just moments before Inspector Fletcher arrives at the Cavendish home.

He follows his brother and sister into the living-room and subjects himself to questioning. Stupid dumb ass cop keeps on talking about the school yard but Tom keeps his cool and defends himself. "Damn cops blame me for every damn thing that goes wrong in this stinkin' town! I don't know nuthin about this kid and that's the God honest truth!"

As soon as the cop gives up and leaves the house Tom leaves the living-room and goes upstairs to his room. He picks up his guitar case from the room's corner, removes the guitar and slides it under his bed. Carrying the case he leaves the house and in the backyard he enters the garden shed. He opens the guitar case and puts the garden spade into it. Closing the case he leaves the shed and begins walking through the yard to the sidewalk at the front of his house. He can't help but notice all the people gathering and milling about on the boardwalk. He increases his pace and soon he is away from the crowd and on the road heading out of town.

He walks for some time and then he sees the sun setting behind the trees. It is beginning to get dark. Tom makes another decision. Turning back he decides to return home. He doesn't want to be out there digging in the dark. He will wait, get some sleep, then go back to his car first thing in the morning.

Early the next day Tom leaves the house. He has his guitar case in hand. By now he can see that the townspeople are arriving ready to be organized into search parties. He quickens his pace. He has to get to his car, do what needs to be done before a search party discovers his vehicle in the woods.

It's a very long walk but at last he can see his car. He approaches it with care but relaxes a little when he feels assured that no one has been around. The car is exactly where and how he had left it.

He opens his guitar case, removes the shovel and is prepared to begin digging Susan Donnelly's grave. He opens the car's back door and shoves the guitar case onto the back seat. Then with the shovel he begins to dig. The spot he chooses for the grave is on the side of the vehicle away from the road. He feels confident no one will see him.

He digs for a long time. At last he feels the hole is deep enough. He rests for a few minutes; then throwing the shovel onto the ground he moves to open the trunk of his car.

He lifts the hood prepared to lift Susan Donnelly's little body out of the trunk. Two startled blue eyes stare back at him.

Susan Donnelly is alive.

Shocked to see that the child is not dead Tom Cavendish freezes in his tracks.

"Get me out of here," Susie pleads. "How did I get in here?"

"Oh, my God! Are you okay kid?"

"I've been sleeping but I'm awake now. Why am I sleeping in your car?"

Thinking fast on his feet Tom replies, "That's what I'd like to know. What are you doing in my car?"

"I don't know," little Suzie cries. "I can't remember."

TWENTY-THREE

TWENTY-THREE:

Police Chief Madison Morris

After his conversation with Annie Benjamin, Inspector Fletcher puts out an all-points bulletin for the capture of Ronald Thompson.

Police Chief Madison Morris and Constable Nick Taylor, with the help of the OPP, had done a good job of keeping the crowd gathered on the boardwalk under control. They divided them all into search teams and sent them off in different directions.

They were walking teams that could cover only so much territory. The Chief decided he would take the cruiser and do a little of his own searching outside the town limits. "Come on with me, Nick."

"Sure Maddy. What you got in mind?"

"These good people have got the search covered within town limits, Nick. Let's you and I drive outside of town a little ways and see what we can see."

"Fletcher and those RCMP fellows are on the go looking for Ronald Thompson. Think he's probably the right target, boss?"

"Probably Nick, but who knows that for sure? I've just got me a hunch. Can't explain and wouldn't bother even if I could but I want to follow the gut feeling I woke up with this morning."

"We know what happened last time you followed your hunches Maddy."

"I know. I know Nick. I was pretty sure I was on the right track with the grandfather."

"Didn't mean to rub salt in the wound, Maddy."

"I know you didn't Nick. No worries. We'll just drive and keep our eyes peeled for anything suspicious looking, okay?"

"Yes, sir."

Tom Cavendish lifts Susan Donnelly out of his car's trunk. "Come on, Susie, I'm going to take you home."

Swooped up in Tom's arms Susie was a very confused little girl. "What's the big hole in the ground for, Tom?"

"That aint nuthin' for you to be concerned about," Tom snapped. "Come on now. In you go," he said as he set her down on the back seat of the car.

Then getting into the driver's seat he tries to calm himself down enough to think straight. Before gunning the engine he had concocted what he thought was a good story. He will take the kid home; tell them he found her wandering beside the road; that he picked her up and brought her home. As long as the kid keeps her mouth shut he will be a hero.

Driving along the road toward town he gets more than a little nervous when he sees the police cruiser coming in the other direction.

*

Madison spots the car coming toward town. "You recognize the vehicle Nick?"

"No, sir."

Madison feels a tightening in his stomach. "Gotta follow my hunch, Nick. Let's stop him and ask a couple questions." He swings his vehicle to the left in this way blocking the oncoming lane.

Tom has no choice but to stop. He recognizes the local cops and he decides he can bluff his way through this. Rolling his window down he shouts, "Hey man! I'm glad I run into you guys."

"You don't say?"

"Yep, you won't believe who I've got here in my car with me. I found the kid! I found Susan Donnelly!"

Maddy and Nick exchange glances. "You don't say," Maddy repeats. "Step out of the car, Tom. Hands high, no monkey business. Step out of the car."

"Hey man! Didn't you hear what I said? I found the kid."

"Out of the car, Tom!"

Tom does as he is ordered. Hands in the air, Maddy swirls him around. "Put your hands on the roof of the vehicle. Keep your gun on him, Nick."

"Yes, sir."

Madison opens the back door of the car and is pleased as punch to see the little girl alive and safe sitting on the back seat. "Hello little girl. What's your name?"

"Susan."

"I'm very happy to see you Susan. What is your last name?"

"Donnelly. I'm Susan Donnelly."

"Come on out of the car now, Susan. We are going to take you home to your mother. Have you ever been in a police car before? We will give you a great ride, sirens and all if you like."

"Why do I have to go in a police car? I didn't do anything wrong."

"No, of course you didn't. But your Mommy has been missing you. We will take you home to her now."

"Tommy is taking me home. Why do I have to go in a police car?" Susie is crying now, feeling very afraid. "Only bad people go in police cars. I didn't do anything bad," she cries.

"Of course you didn't, Susie. We are going to take Tom home too. What were you doing in Tom's car anyway, Susan?"

"I can't remember," she answers.

"Put the cuffs on him, Nick," Maddy shouts. Then to Susan, "Come on, we will take you home now." Opening the back door of the cruiser Madison assists Susan into the car.

Then he joins Nick on the other side of the car. "What's your story, Tom?"

"I told you already. I found the kid wandering at the road side. I picked her up and I was bringing her home. End of story."

"Hmm," is all Maddy has to say about that. "Okay, get in your car and drive straight home. We are right behind you. Don't make any funny moves."

"Geez, even when I am the hero I'm treated like shit by you guys."

"Just get in your car and drive, Tom. The less you say right now the better. We are right behind you."

TWENTY-FOUR

TWENTY-FOUR:

The Final Chapter

Gerald Gagnon opens the front door of number five Crabapple Court when he hears the police cruiser pull into the driveway. He sees the officer assisting the little girl out of the car. "Patricia, Susie is safe. She's home. They've found her!"

"Thank God! Thank God! Thank God!" Patricia shouts. With joy she leaps up from the couch and runs to the window. "My baby is home!"

She rushes to the front door and follows her father outside. Falling to her knees on the front walk she sweeps her little girl into her arms and holds her close. "Oh, Susie, baby. Thank God you are home."

"I had a ride in the police car, Mommy. And they put the sirens on for me too."

"They did? How wonderful! Oh, Susie, thank God you are home."

"If you don't mind, ma'am, maybe we could get inside the house before all the reporters are on top of us here in your front yard," the police chief suggests.

"Oh, yes, of course. Come in! Come in everyone!"

The reporters were approaching. "Maybe not everyone," Gerald shouts. "Get into the house Patricia." To his grand-daughter he smiles, "Welcome home, Susie."

*

Thomas Cavendish is charged with kidnapping. Once the open grave is found in the woods with the garden spade containing his fingerprints nearby and Tom's tire tracks next door to the hole he is arrested. There will be a Court trial but there is no question of his guilt.

When Susan Donnelly tells her mother and the police about the candies Tom gives to the children in the schoolyard he is further charged with drug trafficking.

There is much sadness in number nine Crabapple Court. Tom's father, George, declares, "Always said that boy was no good and that's exactly what he is." Feeling alone in her grief his mother weeps.

Dolores and Robert huddle together. "The kids at school will give me a hard time knowing my big brother is a drug-pusher and a kidnapper," Robert says to his big sister.

"Let's hope it is all blown over by the time we get back to school, Robby. It won't be easy for me in high school either."

The search party is called off. Susan is safe. Inspector Fletcher cancels his search for Ronald Thompson.

Annie Benjamin holds her little Arabella close and prays he will never return to town.

In number three Crabapple Court Doctor Heather Martin breathes a deep sigh of relief. "It was a big lesson learned for me, Ernie," she says to her husband. "I made a huge mistake sedating Patricia so quickly the way I did. I just assumed that Gerald had already contacted the police. Never again will I forget the folly of making assumptions."

"I don't believe you were ever really a suspect in the disappearance, Heather."

"I'm not so sure, Ernie. I'm just glad the whole thing is over and Susie is safely home."

"Yes, I hope I never have to participate in that kind of a search party again. Gotta give the boys credit though, Heather. They were dedicated to helping to find the girl; all three of them."

"Yes, Ernie. We are blessed to have such good sons. I don't know why I tried to prevent them from joining the search party."

"Doesn't matter now. Put it all behind you. Thank God it's over."

In number seven Crabapple Court Marsha Kovacs cries. Her husband Daniel does his best to console her but she is beyond consolation. "They considered me a suspect, Dan. The police actually thought I may have kidnapped that child."

"I'm sorry for what all this has put you through, Marsha. But let's put the past behind us and move forward now."

"That's easy for you to say, Dan. You were never a suspect."

"Marsha, maybe it's time we sat down and discussed the possibility of adopting a child."

"Do you mean that Dan?"

"I mean it."

For the first time in many months Marsha could feel the warmth of a ray of sunshine entering into her life.

"I've made another decision, Dan."

"What's that Marsha?"

"This whole experience has made me realize that it truly is not a good idea for me to be bringing my clients into the home. I'm going to check out finding myself an office downtown."

"Good idea, Marsha. Especially once we have our child it won't be a good idea to be bringing unsavoury characters into her home."

"Our child. Yes, our child. I do love the sound of that, Dan."

In number eleven Crabapple Court Annette Colletti regrets her phone call to Patricia Donnelly. She had truly believed in her heart of hearts that Ronald Thompson was the evil-doer.

She makes a vow to herself that she will not be in such a hurry to jump to conclusions again no matter what the circumstances. It's best to keep out of her neighbour's business and from now on that is exactly what she will do. Her husband, Mario, is right she decides; at least in this regard.

Annette is grateful that her daughters are in good, safe marriages. She wishes the same was true for her housekeeper, Annie Benjamin. She had phoned Annie and was pleased to learn that Ronald had not returned. She prays he never will.

As for Madison Morris and Nick Taylor, they are famous. They are heroes. In all his years as Chief of Police in Fairmont this is the first time Maddy has gained national attention and sees his name hit the headlines of the big Toronto newspapers.

"Susie is Safe Thanks to Police Chief Madison Morris" the Toronto Star shouts while the Globe

and Mail's more sedate headline declares *"Local Drug-pusher Charged in Kidnapping of Susan Donnelly."*

Fairmont's local paper knows what is most important to the residents of Fairmont. Its headline simply states *"Susan Donnelly is Alive and Well."*

Without exception the townspeople are elated. "Knew it was somebody who lived in one of them houses," one says.

"Yep, never doubted it for a minute. Rich kid like that pushing drugs on little children. Hope they hang him!"

"Hanging's too good for the likes of him."

Patricia Donnelly is not the only mother in Fairmont who keeps a closer watch on her child now. Sadly the days of unlocked doors and children playing freely in the schoolyards and public parks are a thing of the past. Patricia Donnelly, like all the mothers in Fairmont, is much wiser now. She is taking no chances. Even though she knows Tom Cavendish will spend a lot of years behind bars, she is making sure there are no more early morning visits to the school yard. "I can't believe one of our neighbours is a drug pusher, Dad."

"They don't wear signs on their backs, Patricia. They can live anywhere; even on Crabapple Court."

It isn't long before life returns to normal in the once again peaceful Town of Fairmont. "Come outside now children. This is a good day to be outside playing."

"Why can't we stay in the house? I want to watch TV," a child complains

And the mother sharpens her eyes as with a new caution she looks up and down the street on which she lives before she says "The fresh air is good for you. Outside you go! But make sure you stay in your own backyard."

"I want to go to the school yard and play on the swings with my friends."

"No way!"

"But Mom."

"No buts about it! Just do as you're told!"

It is summer in Fairmont and the Crabapple trees are in full flower. The delicate colours offered by the fragrant blooms entice the eye of the tourist's camera. The colourful hues are revealed in a spectacular floral display. The flowers are open and they remain like the residents of Crabapple Court; vulnerable to the elements but hopeful of a long and pleasing life.

And life goes on.

About the Author

As a writer I am fulfilled when creating stories, characters, and situations which before never existed outside my imagination.

Crabapple Court is a novella; my latest child to leave the nest. It celebrates its local launch in the fall of 2014.

All my books are available on all Amazon sites. My author's page is found at http://www.amazon.com/author/audreyaustin

Whether you choose one of my novels, a novella or a short story, I hope you will enjoy the read.

We cannot get beyond what we have never been in.

About the Cover Designer

Susan Ruby Krupp

http://yuneekpix.com

Living and freelancing in Elliot Lake, Susan has developed what she affectionately calls "Phollage". It's a combination of photography, painting and digital manipulation that she has explored and developed using tools of the computer. The possibilities are virtually endless, and she's intrigued that the learning curve continues to take her on this fantastic journey. She specializes in portraiture (both people and pets) as well as more mainstream graphic design.

www.ingramcontent.com/pod-product-compliance
Lightning Source LLC
Chambersburg PA
CBHW061327050726
47504CB00013B/1162